Into the Forgotten Kingdom

The Vanguard Series

Book 4

*****

For my family who believes in miracles.

ISBN-13: 978-1534715462 (pbk)
ISBN-10: 1534715460 (pbk)

Contents

CHAPTER 1

The Living Jungle

Taeliah led the way down the trail perched atop her pet vrag. She had placed a saddle carefully between a row of spikes that ran down the animal's back and hung her knapsack across its horns. Truen and Valent followed closely behind the elfin princess on foot.

Taeliah held out the scroll that had been left by the elf that had found the first wish stone. "It says here that we travel east until we come to the Living Jungle." She paused. "I wonder what a Living Jungle is .... The only clue is 'things are not what they appear to be. Be on your guard.'"

"Judging from our luck so far, it can't be anything good," Valent replied.

"You know," Truen piped up, "I can see why no one ever returned with another wish stone. We've traveled miles of rough terrain, climbed mountains, no, make that mountain *ranges*, forged rivers, built bridges across bottomless gorges, battled creatures that I wouldn't have wished on my worst enemy, and survived swarms of dangerous insects, all without even a spark of fire power from me. This is torture!"

"Well, you should have considered the consequences before you stole our wish stone," replied Taeliah.

"We've been over this. We didn't have a choice. Belzar was threatening our friend," Truen answered defensively.

"Just because you have a good reason to do something wrong, doesn't make the wrong thing right," said Taeliah.

"She's got a point, Truen," Valent replied.

Truen just rolled his eyes. His brother had been smitten by Taeliah's beauty the moment he first laid eyes on her. He was hopeless. The witty brother he'd come to know and love had been replaced by a starry-eyed, lovesick pup. Truen wanted his brother back.

"Just, please tell me we are almost there," Truen pleaded.

"The wish stone cave should be on the other side of the jungle," Taeliah replied. "Oh, I see the jungle! It's just up ahead. Come on vrag! Let's be the first ones to the jungle," she said scratching her scraggly mount behind the ears. The vrag snorted and sprinted for the jungle. Valent sped after them while Truen stopped and looked after them for a moment trying to summon strength to his tired bones. With effort, he trotted after them.

By the time Truen caught up to them, Valent was forging a path through the trees with a machete. "This would be so much easier with a little fire power," Truen complained.

"Why don't you take a turn with this, brother?" Valent asked. "You'd be surprised how therapeutic it is."

Truen chuckled. There was the brother he knew. He grabbed the machete and hacked away. Valent jogged back to check on Taeliah who had been delayed at the jungle's entrance. Due to the density of the foliage, she was forced to leave the vrag behind. "Stay here, fella. We won't be long," she promised.

She turned to Valent. "Did you know this guy can travel almost as fast as the speed of light if he has the proper motivation?" she asked.

"And what kind of motivation would he need to do that?" Valent asked.

"Once, I fell down and scratched my knee. He threw me on his back and had me home before I could blink," she replied.

"He's a faithful animal," Valent commented.

"Yes, he is," she agreed reaching up to scratch her pet under the chin. As she did so her long sleeve pulled away from her wrist.

Valent, who seldom took his eyes off Taeliah, noticed thick, brown, dry skin covering her arm. Taeliah had a beautiful fair complexion, so he was more than a little disturbed at the sight. Taeliah turned and followed Valent's gaze to her exposed arm. Their eyes met and Valent quickly looked away, pretending he hadn't seen. Suddenly self-conscious, Taeliah pulled her sleeve down over her arm. Seeing she was uncomfortable, Valent started up a conversation.

"I was hoping you would tell me more about how the elves came to have a wish stone in the first place," he said as the two walked quickly to catch up with Truen.

"Well," she began after double checking to make sure her arms were fully covered, "the first wish stone was found accidentally by an elf named Thael. He kept meticulous notes on his travels. Thank you, Thael." She held up the scroll.

"My people were so excited about the possibilities a wish stone offered they immediately made any wish that popped into their mind. They wanted larger homes, thicker hair, and more friends. However, the elves soon learned that each wish came with a price."

"A price?" Valent interrupted.

"There is no such thing as something for nothing. Many wishes were made before we realized this. We thought—"

"Wait. *We*?" Valent asked.

"Yes, we," Taeliah replied. "I was there. That was two hundred years ago." Reading his thoughts she smiled. "Yes, that makes me two hundred nineteen years old."

"You look ...." Valent began, but was unable to finish his sentence.

Luckily, Truen, who had been listening in on the conversation, came to the rescue. "Let me say what my mute brother is thinking. You look great for your age." He looked at Valent and then corrected himself. "No, make that *fantastic*." Valent reddened at his brother's forthright speech.

Taeliah blushed as well and then continued her story. "An elf who had wished for money soon discovered that another was missing the exact amount he had received. One who wished for love lost a friendship. Another who simply wanted a greener garden stopped the rain from falling on our village for months.

"So you see, there is always a price. But the wishes were made so quickly, that we didn't realize the effects until it was too late. Thael's first wish was that he and his people would live a long time. As soon as he made that wish, our aging pretty much stopped."

"So why is your father so sick, then?" Valent asked. "Shouldn't Thael's wish preserve his life?"

Taeliah hesitated. "My father has lived for a very long time and he has passed beyond the age of a tree."

"What does that have to do with anything?"

"We don't live forever. The original wish was worded 'to live as long as a tree.' Every time the wish stone was used, it grew dimmer. When we realized the danger of using the stone and that there was a limited number of wishes the stone could grant, it was decided to place the stone in the spring to dilute the wishes so many could benefit from them.

"My father has been sick for a long time. The only reason he has been able to live as long as he has, is the healing properties the wish stone brings to the water."

"Not to sound callous," interjected Truen, "but hasn't he lived long enough? Maybe it's time to let him go."

"You don't understand. My father possesses the secret of our survival through his gift of knowing. He has not been well enough to pass this on to me. I desperately wanted to use the wish stone to wish him a longer life, but he wouldn't let me. He didn't want to risk the safety of his people in order for him to be healed. He was beginning to teach me the secret when he got sick. If he dies, we all do."

"Let me get this straight," Truen said fully involving himself in the conversation. "Your father wouldn't let you use the stone to heal him because he's worried about the safety of the elves, but if he dies with his secret untold, you all die anyway?"

"It makes perfect sense to me," Valent defended.

"It's complicated. My father doesn't know the price of a healing wish of this magnitude. He keeps hoping he will heal on his own."

"But what about the wishes in the spring," Valent asked. "I saw you use the stone then to help your father."

"A wilted flower garden is the only consequence there. That is one price we are willing to pay," Taeliah explained.

Truen hacked through a few more vines and the group came into a more open part of the jungle. Vines laden with fruit hung from the trees. The ground was covered with a giant melon patch and the surrounding trees yielded a colorful variety of edibles. "Fruitopia!" Truen shouted. "Finally, something good happens to us. I'm starving."

"Wait, Truen! Remember Thael's warning. It's not what it appears," Taeliah shouted after the Pyrosian but he was already slapping the melons, trying to find one that was ripe.

"I'll go after him," Valent offered and jogged after his brother.

"The key to a good melon is the beestings," Truen explained over his shoulder.

"Beestings?" Valent asked.

"The dark sticky spots on the skin," Truen clarified. "They're actually sugar that has leaked out through the rind of the melon and solidified into sticky globs, but people call them beestings. Tomato, tomoto. Same thing. All I know is they always mean a sweet melon." Truen waded through the vines of the melon patch until he found what he was looking for.

"Look, Valent, this is what I was talking about," Truen said pointing to a large round melon that was almost half his size. He grabbed the melon and attempted to pull it off the vine.

"Truen, I don't know if that's such a good idea. We don't know anything about this place except for the notes in Thael's scroll."

"It's *not* a good idea!" Taeliah shouted in agreement. "It's a terrible idea!"

Just then, the melon in Truen's arms came to life splitting in half to reveal jagged rind teeth. Truen fell back and one of the vines picked him up, lifting him into the air by his feet. "Help!" Truen cried as the vine dangled him over its gaping melon mouth.

"You have to admit this is ironic," Taeliah said to Valent, somewhat enjoying Truen's predicament. The Pyrosian should have heeded her warning and stayed out of the melon patch. "Food eating Truen. It's kinda funny actually."

A vine shot around Valent's leg and Taeliah was no longer smiling. She pulled her trusty bow from her shoulder strap, loaded it with an arrow from her quiver, and shot it at the vine. It dropped Valent who promptly ran out of the patch. He and Taeliah talked as the vine swung Truen first one direction and then the other like a rag doll.

"Heeellllp!" he yelled.

"Maybe we should help him out," Valent suggested.

"Can I watch this just a little longer?" Taeliah begged.

"Okay," Valent chuckled, "but just one more minute." Truen flew across the melon patch until he was thoroughly shaken and the vine was done playing with its food. It began to lower Truen toward its mouth until all that was stopping him from being eaten was his hands on either side of the melon's gaping mouth.

"I know you two are really enjoying this," Truen said quite calmly considering his precarious circumstances, "but I would really appreciate some help."

"Do you both promise to listen to me from now on?" Taeliah asked and Valent readily agreed. Truen, however, was silent for a minute. "Well?" she pressed. "Is there really even a decision here?"

"I'm thinking about it," he said glancing into the melons mouth. "It's seedless. I really like seedless melons."

"Okay, I'm leaving now," Taeliah said turning to go.

"Alright, I'll listen. You have my word." Truen said.

"Deal," replied Taeliah as she fired two arrows at the vine that held Truen suspended. The melon plant squealed and released Truen and he fell to the ground in a heap. No sooner had he hit the ground than the three of them skedaddled out of there. Even Truen had lost his appetite, and that was saying something.

CHAPTER 2

Warnings

Jonuke stood in front of a tall stone tower. He looked up and saw a single window at the top. He became aware of a faint melody. He climbed the winding stairs and entered a large room.

A woman with long dark hair in a flowing sea green dress sat near the window singing. She didn't see Jonuke come in and continued her sad song.

Remember the days we were happy?
Remember the days of yore?
We danced, and played and loved and laughed
But now those days are no more

He was the love of my life

And he was the apple of my eye
No family was ever more blissful than we
If only I'd said 'goodbye'....

The woman's song ended and she began to cry softly. Jonuke took a step toward her. Startled the woman sat up and looked at her unexpected visitor.

"Jonuke! What are you doing here? How did you find me?" Jonuke recognized the woman immediately. It was his mother, Linayah. She rushed over to Jonuke but didn't touch him. "It doesn't matter. You're here! How I've missed you!" She clasped her hands in front of her chin.

Tears streamed down her face as she looked him up and down and said, "Let me look at you. How you've grown! You are a man now and so much like your father...." She sniffed back the emotion that readily came to the surface at the mention of Londor.

"Where are we?" asked Jonuke. "Is this Heaven?"

"No, my dearest. It is much closer to the opposite," she replied.

"So you're alive?" Jonuke asked. She nodded. "What is this place?"

"Where I am doesn't matter. I must be here for now, but if you should ever need me, I will be there."

Jonuke thought about that for a minute. "You've come to me before, in dreams, haven't you?"

She nodded. "Many times, but I can only come when you need me the most."

It all made sense. He remembered now that she had visited him many times before. She had helped him heal his father, she had healed him when he was hurt, she had helped him find his way home once when he was lost. He now recognized that it was her voice that had guided him so many times when he didn't know what to do.

"There is something I must tell you. You must keep your identity a secret. If Dendrid discovers who you are—"

"Dendrid?" Jonuke interrupted.

"The Karakan," Linayah corrected. "If he knows you are the Vanguard, I will not be able to shield you any longer."

"Shield me?" Jonuke asked.

"I have always known you are special, Jonuke. I placed a shield over the Darke Forest, so that he could not see you, to keep you safe until you discovered who you are.

"Den—the Karakan has recently obtained a powerful object. You must find the Crown of Rulers for it alone can stand against the Karakan's new power. You must find each of the crown's nine missing gems, hidden by each of the nine kingdoms, from those who would abuse the crown's power, for he who wears the crown, rules Galvadon."

"But how will I find the gems?" asked Jonuke.

"You have the first, given to you by Mahlneer, the last great ruler of Galvadon. It will lead you to the rest," his mother explained.

"Linayah!" echoed a deep voice that shook the tower. "Where are you, Linayah?"

"You must go now, dear one. I cannot let him find you here," she said anxiously.

"Come with me! I can get you out of here," Jonuke pleaded.

She shook her head sadly. "You mustn't ..." her voice broke. She closed her eyes and collected herself for a moment. "Jonuke, you mustn't tell your father about me."

"You can't ask that of me, Mother," Jonuke reasoned tenderly. "We don't keep things from each other."

"It is imperative for his safety and yours that you do not. Even now you are in great danger. Please, Jonuke. Promise me." Jonuke had to agree. She was desperate and he had to trust that she had a good reason. "Thank you. Now wake up. Wake up, Jonuke."

Jonuke sat up in his hammock in a cold sweat. Londor had just entered the room with a torch in his hand. "Are you alright, son? You were calling out in your sleep."

Jonuke told him about the dream but left out the woman's identity and the fact that she was in trouble. Londor looked at Jonuke intently, as if he could sense

Jonuke was keeping something from him. Jonuke feared he would ask him questions that he had promised not to answer. He didn't think he could lie to his father.

"What did she look like? The woman in your dream," Londor asked. Jonuke gave a vague description that could fit almost any woman. His father didn't say anything and seemed to accept Jonuke's description.

Londor stood to leave. "Get some sleep. We've got a big day tomorrow." He went to the door and paused. "Did the woman seem happy? The woman from your dream, I mean. Was she happy with her life? "

Jonuke felt very uncomfortable. Did he know? How was he supposed to answer that question when his mother was clearly in some kind of trouble? "She seemed happy enough," Jonuke lied and immediately felt terrible about it. "Why do you ask?" he probed nervously.

"Something about what you told me about her keeps nagging at me. Her familiarity with you perhaps? You said you've never met her before?"

"Not that I can remember." Jonuke answered honestly.

"It's probably nothing then." He smiled and disappeared down the hallway, but there was a look of sadness in his eyes.

*****

Jonuke and Scithe had been out hunting all day long and arrived home just before dark that night. Scithe was laughing, "No, I've definitely learned to listen to my Drek guide."

"If you hadn't, I wouldn't hesitate to hit you with another bantham barb," Jonuke teased.

The smile melted off Scithe's face as he recalled their last assignment together. He and Jonuke hadn't been getting along when Scithe was "accidently" hit with a poison dart. His whole arm went numb and he could have died if Jonuke didn't come to the rescue with a remedy. "Wait ... that was you? You did that on purpose?" Scithe said with an astonished look. "I didn't know you were capable of such cruelty."

"Admit it, bro, you deserved it," Jonuke said punching him on the shoulder.

"True, but still ... that was harsh," Scithe replied, rubbing his shoulder at the painful memory. "I'll be extra careful to stay on your good side from now on. For my own safety," he added.

Londor and Renden heard the boys come in and met them in the kitchen. "What did you bring us for dinner?" Renden asked.

"We have several dweedle birds and—" Jonuke stopped mid-sentence when an old book suddenly materialized and fell on the dining table with a *smack*. "The Book of Truth," Jonuke said with astonishment. The book had a mind of its own and appeared sporadically, but when it did, it was usually about to reveal an important event.

At Scithe's confused look he explained, "This is what Truen, Yondel and I went after during that glup duty assignment. It tells the past, present, and the possible future. And if it's chosen now to appear, there is a really good reason."

They all watched in amazement as the pages flipped of their own volition and then stopped suddenly. The words flew off the page and formed a glowing scene in the air high above the book.

Scithe's face went pale at the image of his father, Silvane, and a woman arguing. "Is that my ... mother? She's been gone for a long time now. How does it know about my family?" he asked.

"The Book of Truth records all of Galvadon's history. We're all in there," Jonuke explained.

They watched Silvane's cruel treatment of the woman and her decision to leave her husband. It was night and she woke the young Scithe from his sleep and tried to take him with her. But Silvane had awakened and took Scithe from her. He grabbed at her arm but she bolted out of the house and vanished into the night.

The scene changed. It showed an aerial view of Aeris and then zoomed into a single house. Inside was the older version of Scithe's mother. Scithe took a step closer to the image of his mother. "She's alive? My father told me she was dead. What's she doing in Aeris?" The woman lay in bed and looked ill. A girl was sitting next to the bed tending to her. They couldn't see her face, but she was singing.

Scithe recognized the song immediately. "My mother used to sing me that song every night when she put me to bed. How does she know that song?"

The girl turned to get a glass of water and Scithe thought she looked familiar. "Don't worry, Mother. We'll find a cure," she said reassuringly and then the scene changed.

"I have a sister?" Scithe whispered.

The next scene showed Scithe and Yondel. She was handing him a plant. "Now let's get this to your mother," she said and the scene faded.

"How is that even possible?" Scithe said to Jonuke. "She hates my guts!"

"Like I said, the book shows a probable future. It's up to you to make it happen," Jonuke explained.

Suddenly, the pages began to turn rapidly and then stopped as quickly as they had started. "It's never done that before," Jonuke said.

"Maybe it has something more to show us," Londor suggested.

Jonuke's father was right. Another scene unfolded before their eyes. This time it showed the Karakan speaking to one of his Elite. "I've had enough of that Hydran councilman, Oregg! Dispose of him at once! And then disband the council. All will obey me and only me from this point forward." He held up the Master's Blade.

"The Karakan has the Master's Blade?" Jonuke gasped. "How?!" He remembered his mother had told him that the Karakan had become more powerful.

The Elite were shown taking Oregg and his family away leaving the house eerily quiet and dark. The scene closed.

"I have to get to Yondel and warn her," Jonuke said.

"If the Karakan has the Master's Blade, then we have little hope left," Londor concluded.

The pages began turning again and produced yet another scene. "I'm afraid to look," said Scithe. "Does this thing ever reveal good news?"

"Nope," replied Jonuke.

The book showed the Elite raiding the Darke Forest. "Round up all the rebels. Make them tell us who the Vanguard is." It showed a Freemen getting captured and revealing Jonuke's true identity as the Vanguard. The next scene showed Jonuke had been captured and was turned to stone and placed on display in the Citadel. The inscription at his feet read, "For all who question the Karakan as Supreme Ruler of all the Land."

An involuntary shiver ran up Jonuke's spine. "I told you not to look," Scithe reminded. "How much time do we have until this comes true?"

"Little," Jonuke replied.

"We must act quickly," Londor asserted. "Scithe, you warn Oregg and enlist Yondel to find the medicine for your mother. Jonuke, you said Mahlneer told you to find the Crown of Rulers and its missing gems. Now that the Karakan has the Master's Blade, that is our best chance. It seems the woman from your dream knows you pretty well, Jonuke."

Jonuke looked away. He couldn't face Londor's penetrating gaze. "But what about you and Renden?" Jonuke asked.

"The Freemen are back in Galvadon. Great timing, right?" said Renden.

"Do they know you are the Vanguard?" Scithe asked. "They won't talk will they?"

"They know. When they are captured, they won't have to talk," Londor replied. "The Karakan will see the truth through their fear."

"But they can't tell something they don't know. Renden went to a drawer and removed two golden orbs. "Your father and I will make sure your identity remains a secret, Jonuke."

"Scithe," Jonuke said, "we both know Yondel is going to have a hard time trusting you. Don't give up. Tell her the truth and she'll come around. And I need you to give Granny an important message. Tell her that I'm on the run and that it's time to carry out operation 'tough love.'" At Scithe's questioning glance, he replied, "She'll know what I mean."

Jonuke looked meaningfully at Scithe, Renden, and Londor. Each nodded their silent goodbyes as Londor opened the door and looked into the forest. The sun had set yet the sounds of night were unnaturally absent. It was eerily quiet.

"It appears we have even less time than we thought. The Elite are already in the forest. "Run, Jonuke! Run!"

CHAPTER 3

Secret Keepers

R enden and Londor snuck through the trees toward the Drek settlements. "Of all the times to come home for a visit, they choose now!" Renden complained.

"They've been gone quite a while. A visit was well overdue," Londor replied remembering how much he had missed Jonuke all the years he was a prisoner in the Silver Lake.

"This raid means that somehow the Karakan knows the Vanguard is in Galvadon," Renden whispered. "I don't know how, but he knows. We can't let him learn that Jonuke is the Vanguard .... No matter what happens to us."

Londor nodded solemnly. There were quite a few Freeman and this was no game. He and Renden were going to have to wipe all of their memories before a single man was caught. The odds were not in their favor. They were up against an unknown number of Elite and there were only two of them. From what he knew of the Karakan, he'd have an army of Elite combing the forest for the Vanguard.

"When I told the Freemen about Jonuke, I knew something like this was a possibility," said Renden. "I hoped it wouldn't come to this but I prepared for this scenario just in case." He held up one of the secret keepers. "Secret keeper, Londor is your new owner. Guard his secrets like you have guarded mine." He placed the sphere in Londor's hand. "You start at the north and I'll go south. We'll finish up somewhere in the middle."

"Where can the Drek hide after we've wiped their memories?" Londor asked. "The forest is swarming with guards."

"Let's have them meet at the Freemen's hideout," Renden replied. He hesitated for a moment feeling the gravity of the situation. "We have to remove all memory of the Vanguard or—?

"There is no 'or'," Londor interrupted. "We're all in. Jonuke is depending on us and the future of Galvadon depends upon him. We have no choice but to succeed."

With that, the men went their separate ways and disappeared into the night.

Renden traveled quickly through the forest. He knew the Darke Forest much better than the Elite did. He hoped this advantage would be enough to win the day. In a short time, he managed to warn all the Drek on the south side.

Roc's house was the last before he would rendezvous with Londor at the safe house. Renden knew he had been lucky. He'd seen several Elite but none had seen him. He had been very careful though. Much depended upon him reaching the Freemen before the Elite.

Renden scouted the perimeter of Roc's premises to make sure the coast was clear before he approached his friend's home. He snuck up to the back entrance and quietly turned the knob.

A dark figure grabbed him from behind and held a knife to his throat. "It's rude to just walk into a man's house without knockin'," came a gruff voice.

"True," Renden replied, "unless a man is in an awful hurry to let his friends know the Elite are raiding the forest for Freemen."

"Elite?" Roc released his friend and the two hurried into the house. "Is that what has the forest so quiet tonight?"

Renden nodded. "The Karakan is searching for the Vanguard. I have to wipe all memory of him before they find us."

"You don't have to tell me twice. Let me get Crusty and we can do a two-fer," Roc suggested.

"You don't need to get anybody," Crusty growled. "I could hear you two yakin' clear across the house. You'd think you were tryin' to attract the bad guys. Now quit your jawin' and get on with it. Time's a wastin'."

Renden held out the small golden ball and twisted it gently. The ball sprouted a four pronged propeller and sprang into the air. It sped around Roc and Crusty gaining speed until it was just a blur.

Roc nodded at Crusty and the men spoke in unison, "Take all memory of the Vanguard." Their memories, in the form of a fine glittering mist, rose from the tops of their heads and the secret keeper syphoned them up like a vacuum cleaner. As soon as the memories were safe inside the sphere, it floated over to Renden's palm and became still.

The two Freemen looked at Renden as he put the keeper in his pocket. "Renden, what brings you here this time of night?" Roc asked a little befuddled by the experience. Renden knew enough about the workings of the secret keeper not to be worried. General confusion was normal, but only the memories that the men spoke were transferred to the secret keeper.

Just then the front door was kicked in. "Search the home!" commanded a gruff voice.

"Get the family into the tunnel," Renden whispered urgently as the men rushed to gather Roc's wife and children.

The Elite stormed the house and searched every room but they found no one. The Elite in charge punched the wall in frustration. "Gone again?! It's like they knew we were coming! We haven't laid eyes on a single Drek tonight! Search the house again. I want to know where all these Drek have gone.

"You, Pyrosian, light the house so we don't miss anything. The rest of you go over this house with a fine tooth comb for any evidence pointing to where they went. Move!"

The Elite spread out across the home and searched every nook and cranny of every room until a guard shouted, "Captain, I found something."

The Elite followed the guard down into the basement of the home. He walked over to a dirt wall lined with several wooden barrels. He lifted the lid off one of the barrels and the captain thrust a torch into it and looked inside. The bottom of the barrel was missing and there was a tunnel that led underneath the home.

The captain kicked the barrel over. "Aerisian, notify the other squads that we've found the rebels."

*****

Londor heaved a huge sigh of relief upon seeing Renden bring Roc's family into the Freemen's hideout. They had miraculously managed to gather every last Drek to the safety of the hidey-hole.

Renden went to the front of the room. "Thank you all for your cooperation. We knew this day would come eventually. We'll stay here tonight until the Elite have given up the search and then move out in the morning. Our best chance long term is the underground gnome village where the Freemen have been staying."

There was a murmur in the room about how long they would be required to stay there. Shouldn't they defend their home? Renden realized that they had no memory, no hope of the Vanguard anymore. "This will not be a permanent situation. Let us stay there for a time until we can make further plans. The Drek saw the wisdom in this and started to make their families as comfortable as possible.

Renden walked over to Londor. "We did it!" he shouted hugging his brother merrily. "We accomplished the impossible. No one knows about the Vanguard but us."

"Then we aren't quite finished," Londor replied as Renden nodded and took out his keeper.

"You know once we do this we won't be able to help Jonuke," he said.

"It's up to him now. We've done all we can," Londor replied as Renden sent his keeper into the air. "Take all memory of the Vanguard," they said in unison. The keeper managed to take in Renden's memory, but then the room started to shake violently. The keeper fell to the ground and Londor's memory fell back into his mind.

"Elite!" Renden gasped. "They've found us!"

Londor looked at Renden and went white. "I still know who the Vanguard is," he whispered.

"The who?" Renden asked as one of the walls dissolved into a pile of rocks

Silvane stepped into the room. "Bind them all. Don't let any of the rebels escape." He walked over to Londor and Renden. "You two have been busy tonight. We hadn't found a single rebel all night ... until now. And now I see that you have rounded them all up for me. You have my deepest gratitude."

Spying the secret keeper on the ground, a guard said, "Look what I found, Captain!"

As he reached for the object, Silvane shouted a warning, "Don't!" But it was too late.

"Ahhh!" yelped the guard as he cradled his singed fingers. His Hydran partner waited for the nod from Silvane before shifting an ice cube to sooth his burn.

Shifting a rock into a pair of tongs, Silvane picked up the orb. It burned white with heat. "This is a secret keeper. If I'm guessing correctly, and I always do, these men have wiped all memory of the Vanguard's identity. The question is, how did they know we were coming?

"I do believe, the Karakan will be very pleased with the outcome of our search and very interested in 'speaking' with these two in particular." He gave the men a shove into the tunnel. "Gather up the rest and bring them back to the Citadel immediately!"

*****

The Karakan waited impatiently for the return of his men. He had to snuff out this Vanguard problem before it got any worse. Galvadon was his now and he wouldn't put up with any trouble makers. When Silvane returned with every Drek from the Darke Forest he was very pleased.

"Line them up!" the Karakan ordered. He walked down the line of Freemen looking at each of them with disgust.

"Show me your hands!" he commanded. Confused, the Drek slowly brought out their hands in front of them. "Silvane, have your men check them for any jewelry ... rings in particular."

"Elite, do as the Karakan commands. Check their hands." The Elite rushed to obey the order. "They have no jewelry, Great Karakan," one guard reported.

"No, that would've been too easy," the Karakan replied calmly. Then whirling on the nearest Drek, which just so happened to be Crusty, he said, "What do you know of the Vanguard?"

"The what now?" asked Crusty with a perplexed look.

"The Vanguard you fool!" the Karakan shouted.

"Can't say I've ever heard that word before," he replied. "But if I find out what happened to your friend, the Vandergood, I'll be sure to let you know."

"He's not my friend, you idiot!" the Karakan shouted.

"Their memories have been wiped, Sir. We found one of them in possession of a secret keeper," Silvane explained.

"A secret keeper?! A secret keeper?!" the Karakan raged and then his eyes came to rest on Londor and his countenance brightened perceptibly. "Silvane, you didn't tell me you caught Londor."

"I said we captured all the Drek, Great Karakan," Silvane replied.

"Well, well, well. The great Londor," said the Karakan. "He who is said to be but a mere shadow in the forest has been captured. Maybe he has some information about the Vanguard," the Karakan said as he walked toward him. "Is that fear I am sensing, Londor? Good. That will give me full access to all you know. Won't that be interesting? How I've looked forward to this moment."

Londor was very aware of the fact that he had the information that would betray his son to his greatest enemy. All they had done tonight would be for nothing if he couldn't get that memory out of his head. He carefully removed the secret keeper from his pocket and nudged Renden.

Renden peered down at the keeper and then at Londor. Maybe it was because they were brothers, or maybe Renden had just gotten lucky, but he knew exactly what his brother wanted. Londor had a memory that he needed to be erased and he wanted Renden to create a distraction before the Karakan and his evil- mind- reading ways got to him.

Renden stepped out of the lineup. "Great Karakan," he bowed deeply. "I have some very important information for you."

Silvane grabbed Renden and shoved him back in line. "How dare you address the Karakan, Drek."

"No, Silvane, let this one speak. He says he has information. What do you know?" the Karakan asked intently.

Renden cleared his throat. "I have heard of this Vandergood fellow."

The Karakan's eyes narrowed. "Vanguard," he corrected.

"Of course, Vanguard, that's what I meant. I have overheard some of my fellow Drek discussing this very subject," Renden stalled. "I've compiled all the information into ... a poem... yes, a poem that I'd like to recite for you now.

The Vanguard is a silly fellow
His antics make the Karakan bellow
Some say he is tall
Others say short
But me, I just say he's ... neat.

"Neat?! That's the information you have for me—" A strange glow in the line of prisoners caught the Karakan's eye.

As soon as Renden had started talking and the Karakan's attention had shifted to his brother, Londor carefully stepped behind another Drek and sent the secret keeper into the air.

"Guards! Stop him! Take the secret keeper before it captures his knowledge of the Vanguard!" But it was too late. Londor had just finished wiping all memory of the Vanguard just as Renden finished reciting his poem. The keeper floated lazily to the ground and a guard obediently picked it up.

"Ahh!" he yelped as he blew on his burning fingers.

The Karakan stormed over to Londor. "Tell me who the Vanguard is! Tell me!"

"I wouldn't tell you even if I could," Londor smiled dumbly.

"Silvane, find a way to extract memories out of that thing!" the Karakan commanded.

"But it can't be done—" Silvane started.

"Find a way!" the Karakan bellowed.

"Yes, Great Karakan," Silvane replied.

"Take the rebels to the center of town and put them in the stocks. I want an example made of them. Make a sign that reads "Traitors to the Crown.""

"But you don't have a crown," Silvane reasoned.

"Make- the- sign!" the Karakan thundered. The Elite took the Drek from the room leaving the Karakan alone. "I was this close to knowing the identity of the Vanguard!" he spat, pinching two fingers together. "This close!"

CHAPTER 4

A Late-Night Visitor

"Why didn't you tell me about my parents sooner?" Yondel asked Granny.

"Quite honestly, I didn't want things to change," Granny replied. "We were a happy family and I didn't want you to lose a father or my son to lose his daughter."

Oregg piped up, "I couldn't bear to have my little girl's heart broken. I wanted to protect you from that, and I had almost convinced myself that I was the only father you ever had." There was a sad look in his eyes. "What good could it do?"

Yondel nodded her understanding of their reasoning. It had brought her pain to know that she had lost a father, but it had also healed her, healed her from the loss of her mother. She couldn't stand seeing Oregg so sad. She leaned over and hugged him tenderly. "You will always be my father," she said. "I love you more than any daughter has loved her father."

"That's all I need to know," he said cheering up considerably. He kissed her lightly on the head. "I'm off to bed."

After he had gone, Yondel whispered to Granny, "I do wish I could remember my mother and father, Keldan. I think that would bring me peace."

"Well, I was waiting for the right time to give you this." She disappeared into another part of the house and returned with a silver handled hairbrush. "This is a gift from your mother."

"My mother?" Yondel said taking the brush reverently from her grandmother. "It's beautiful." Turning it carefully in her hands, she examined it closely admiring the intricate design on the handle.

"It's more than it appears. Here, let me show you." She took the brush from her granddaughter and began to stroke Yondel's long dark hair. Yondel closed her eyes, relaxing and enjoying the gentle caress of the brush strokes. Her mind drifted back in time to a long forgotten memory from her infancy.

In the memory, Yondel was sitting on a swing that hung from a tree at her home in Palean. She was swinging back and forth, back and forth, gently at first and then higher, squealing with delight. She saw her mother smiling at her pretending to grab her toes. How she loved her mother! She remembered the feelings of safety and security and her mother's radiating love.

Yondel became aware that she was being pushed on the swing. But if her mother was in front of her then who …? She turned around and discovered her father, Keldan, grinning widely at her as he pushed her higher and higher into the air. He came around the front of the swing to join her mother and held out his hands to Yondel.

"Jump, Yondel! I'll catch you!" Yondel sprang fearlessly from the swing into her father's arms feeling the exhilaration of love and connectedness with her family.

The memory ended and Yondel turned to Granny and caught her hand with tears welling up in her eyes. "Did you see your mother?" Granny asked tenderly.

"And my father," she added. "We were so happy."

"They loved you dearly Yondel, and they wanted you to know that. They must have suspected you would one day be separated."

"Can I see more?" Yondel implored.

"As many as you like, dear. As many as you like," Granny replied. She so much enjoyed the delight in Yondel's countenance. Granny began to once again stroke Yondel's hair with the brush.

Yondel's next memory was of her mother and father pushing her in a stroller while they laughed and talked. Every now and then Keldan would point to an object and say its name for Yondel's benefit.

"Flower," he said as he plucked a blossom and placed it in Yondel's grasping fingers. "Can you say 'flower'?"

Yondel replied obediently, "Flow-uh."

"Did you hear that?" he said proudly to a passing stranger.

"Now, Yondel, there is something you must know about your father," her mother began. "He may have a small problem with bragging," she teased.

"It's not bragging!" Keldan replied, playing along. "It's simply sharing the truth about my amazing little girl, very loudly, with everyone I meet."

"Bragging," her mother whispered to her and the memory faded.

Granny continued to brush and a new memory started. In it, Yondel was lying in bed and her father was tucking her in. He began to sing her a lullaby that was now familiar to Yondel, but this time there were more verses. He sang about how he and Yondel's mother had met. Then the song took on a sad tone as he sang about their possible parting and that he might not see her grow into adulthood.

He stopped singing and smiled at his little one who was beginning to doze off and brushed a strand of hair away from her face and whispered, "Yondel, I am about to tell you something that you must always remember." Yondel watched as his lips continued to move but she could no longer hear his voice. The image of her father began to blur before her eyes until she could no longer make him out.

"Granny?" Yondel started.

"Yes, my love?"

"Something's wrong," Yondel explained. "I can't see him anymore." Granny stopped stroking and Yondel turned and looked at her expectantly. "He started to tell me something important, something he said I should always remember, but I couldn't hear him and then he faded away. What happened? Why can't I see more?"

"As long as I brush your hair you should still be able to see into your past. I don't understand ... unless ..."

"Unless what?" Yondel prompted.

"Unless you are holding some kind of resentment."

"Are you saying that I'm upset with my parents, so I don't want to remember them? That isn't true," Yondel said defensively.

"It's not a resentment for your parents necessarily," Granny explained. "It could be unresolved anger or blame for anyone or anything. This kind of pent up emotion prevents you from accessing the sweet joyful memories of your past. Until you can work through these negative emotions, your ability to access memories of the past will be limited."

"How do I clear it out?" Yondel asked. "I don't feel resentful right now...."

"No, to this point you have been unaware of the unresolved feelings you have been holding on to, but now you are awake to the problems they can cause. Can you think of no one for whom you hold a grudge? Anyone at all?"

Yondel thought for a minute. She didn't have any enemies. In fact, she got along with people very well. But then her subconscious mind found the answer on its own. The Galvadonian Games played back in her mind and how she had been cheated out of the title of champion by Scithe Silvane. She loathed him. He had made her life miserable from their first meeting at the Games. Granny was right. She definitely had some unresolved anger there. And then there was a knock at the door.

"I wonder who that could be so late at night," Granny wondered aloud as she went to the door. Yondel followed her out of curiosity. Granny peeked through the peep hole and turned to her granddaughter with eyes wide with astonishment. "Yondel, you won't believe who it is!" Yondel shrugged and looked back at her Granny with curiosity. "Scithe Silvane!" Granny declared.

Granny threw the door open wide as Yondel simply stood there in shocked disbelief. "Welcome to our home, Scithe. What brings you to Hydra this evening?"

Yondel couldn't believe Granny was being nice to him. She abhorred the Elite just as much as she did. And then it dawned on her. Granny knew! Granny knew that Scithe was the one she resented. It *was* pretty obvious. Granny had a plan up her sleeve that involved Scithe and she was intentionally buttering him up.

"Judging from the look on Yondel's face," Scithe began, "I know I'm the last person in Galvadon you want to talk with. And with good reason. I'm not saying you don't have good reasons. You do," he babbled nervously. "But if you just let me explain before slamming the door in my face—"

"Nonsense! We would never do that to a visitor!" Granny exclaimed. "Would we, Yondel?" She looked over at Yondel and then revised her comment. "Well, *I* wouldn't do that to a visitor. In fact, we were just talking about you. Weren't we, Yondel?" Yondel just stared blankly still not believing this was happening. "Would you like to come in?" Granny asked graciously.

Scithe looked awkwardly at Yondel, but she wouldn't look back at him. Scithe smiled nervously. "Are you sure that it is alright? I can say what I need to say out here if you would prefer."

"No guest of mine will be left standing on the door-step. Come in, come in!" she repeated grabbing his arm and pulling him into the sitting room. "Would you like to sit down?" Granny offered. Scithe nodded and sat down on the chair furthest from Yondel who was send-ing fiery darts at him with her eyes.

"You look hungry, Scithe dear. Can I offer you some soup?" Granny's eyes twinkled when Scithe did a double take. He shook his head vigorously in the negative. "Oh, come now. This is the good stuff. I'm fresh out of dish-water," she encouraged.

"Dishwater? That was dishwater? No wonder it tasted so bad," Scithe said grimacing at the memory. "No, I think I'll have to pass on the soup, but thank you for your hospitality." Then remembering what brought him to the Oregg home in the first place, he said, "Is your father home?"

"He's already retired for the evening," Granny ex-plained, "but I can take a message down for him."

"It's quite urgent," Scithe pressed. "Would you wake him please?"

"Yondel, go and get your father. While I entertain our guest," Granny suggested.

Yondel rose slowly never taking her eyes off Scithe. Oh, how she despised him! Resentment wasn't a strong enough word for what she felt for him. Out of respect for her Granny, she did as she was told.

Oregg entered the room sleepy-eyed and yawning. Upon seeing who his evening guest was, he became suddenly awake. "Scithe Silvane? I heard you were dismissed from the Elite banished from Galvadon. What are you doing here?"

"Yes, I was and knowing that will only add to the veracity of what I am about to tell you. I risk much in coming here tonight."

"Yes, you do. Out with it, boy. What's the matter?" Oregg boomed.

"I have learned that the Karakan means you harm. He has already dispatched the Elite to bring you back to the Citadel. You must leave here at once," Scithe asserted.

"And how have you come by this knowledge?" Oregg asked.

"Since banishment, Jonuke of Londor has graciously taken me into his home. This evening, I saw the Book of Truth for the first time and it warned us of the Karakan's plan," Scithe explained. "Just to be safe, I would evacuate the whole family. From what I know of the Karakan, he will not hesitate to use your family to get to you."

Yondel's eyes narrowed. She did not like the sound of her friend's name on his lips. How dare he claim to be Jonuke's confidant!

Scithe looked at Yondel. "Jonuke knew you would struggle with me delivering this message. He said you would believe me if I reminded you that the Sage promised the Book of Truth would one day save your father's life and that day is today."

Yondel's jaw dropped. How could he know that? "I don't know what game you are playing, but there is no way I am about to believe you are Jonuke's ... *friend*." Just the thought made her gag.

"He's given enough evidence for me," said Granny.

"For me as well," Oregg agreed. "If there is any chance that my family is in danger, I am willing to risk a night's discomfort just in case."

"There is something more," Scithe began looking at Yondel out of the corner of his eye. He explained that his mother was sick and that he needed Yondel to help him find the remedy to cure her.

"You're kidding, right?" Yondel asked.

"What symptoms did your mother have?" Granny asked.

"She looked tired and pale and had dark circles under her eyes," Scithe replied.

"You've just described the symptoms of every illness out there," Yondel exploded.

"She's right," Granny agreed. "Was there anything else more definitive?"

Scithe thought for a moment. "The veins in her hands were pronounced and seemed to have a purplish hue."

"That's sipro fever. Rare but I've seen it before. The good news is that the cure can be found at the top of Hydra's tallest mountain peak. The bad news, honey," she turned to Yondel, "is that he will need you to go with him."

Yondel looked from her father to Granny. "You two can't seriously believe what this guy is saying. This is Scithe Silvane, aka Spike, Cheat, Bully...."

Granny took Yondel aside. "We know who he is, honey. Your resentment is clouding your judgment of this boy. Something about him has changed. We can trust him."

"Who are you and what have you done with my Granny?" Yondel asked.

Granny chuckled, "Besides, this will give you the perfect opportunity to work through your resentment for the boy. You want to remember your parents, don't you?" Yondel nodded slowly. "Good! Then we're in agreement." She steered Yondel back into the sitting room. "Scithe, we're in business," Granny declared.

Scithe smiled awkwardly. "Thank you."

Just then there was a loud knock at the door. "Councilman Oregg!" a voice called out. "The Karakan requests that you report to the Citadel at once!"

"I have an escape tunnel just for times like these," Granny whispered lifting the rug and revealing a trap door. She lifted the handle. "Into the tunnel! I'll take care of the Elite."

Scithe shivered involuntarily. "Poor souls. They don't even know what's coming."

Granny chuckled and then said seriously, "Scithe, keep her safe."

"You can count on me," he replied.

"I know or I wouldn't have let her go with you in the first place," Granny replied.

"Oh, I almost forgot," Scithe said. "Jonuke told me to tell you he had to leave Galvadon and to go ahead with the plan...operation tough love."

Granny's eyes sparkled. "Message received loud and clear. Now go! Quickly." She closed the trap door and smoothed the rug neatly back in place and then went to the closet and retrieved a duffle bag.

"What is that?" Oregg asked. "Shouldn't we be following them into that tunnel?"

"Nope. My little bag of disguises here is going to save you from those thugs out there. Now put this on and grab the rake on the side of the house and look busy."

Granny handed her son a skull cap and then shifted a large pool of water on the doorstep.

"What are you doing?" Oregg asked as he stuffed his bushy red mane of hair into the skull cap and headed for the back door.

"This is war son," Granny replied with a glint in her eye.

CHAPTER 5

Don't Mess With Granny II

"Open at once in the name of the Karakan," bellowed the Elite.

Granny, careful to avoid the puddle she had made, swung the door open. She smiled brightly. "Well what a wonderful surprise! Visitors! And Elite no less. What a delight!"

"We are here for your son, Councilman Oregg."

Granny's face fell. "Oh what a shame! Oregg has gone out for an evening walk," she said. "But he should be home any minute. Why don't you come in and wait for him?"

"Ma'am, our orders are to search the premises," Flynn said gruffly. When Scithe had been decommissioned, Flynn, as a runner up in the Games, had been called to join the Elite in his place. He had earned his position as squad leader and was anxious to prove himself in order to be promoted to captain.

"By all means," Granny replied beckoning the men to come into the house. Flynn strode into the room and promptly slipped on the large puddle of water that Granny had thrown on the floor. He hit the ground with a *thud*.

"Oh, my, my, my! I am so sorry!" Granny apologized struggling to help the tall Aerisian to his feet, but her hand seemed to slip repeatedly and he hit the ground again and again. "I just finished mopping the floor and I guess it's still a little wet."

Flynn looked at the small ocean he was sitting in and thought the floor was a full on health hazard, not just a little wet. He waved Granny's 'helpful' hand away and got to his feet. He resisted rubbing his bruised backside even though it ached something terrible. He wasn't about to let his men see him nursing his wounds.

"You two check the upper level and the rest search the grounds." Flynn signaled his squad. The men split up to carry out their orders.

"Oh, I'd better check on things up there," Granny said in a fretful tone. "We weren't expecting visitors, you know, and I'm afraid it's a bit of a mess. We've already had one injury tonight. I'd feel awful if those boys were to trip over something in the dark." With that, Granny scurried up the stairs.

Flynn thought it best to check the ground level himself while keeping an eye on the front door in case someone tried to sneak out. He heard the footsteps of his men and the opening and closing of doors as they did a thorough search of the second floor. And then he heard a *crash* followed by a *thud*.

Flynn went to the foot of the stairs. "What's going on up there?" he called.

"It's alright, Sir. It was just an accident. Just a few things I didn't see in the hallway—"

The guard was interrupted by another crash. Flynn heard Granny's voice full of regret, "I am so terribly sorry! I didn't see you there! Are you alright? Come with me, dear. Let me get you one of my old-fashioned remedies for that goose-egg. The swelling will go down in no time."

An "oof!" was followed by a low groan.

"Did I do that?" Granny gasped. "I was just trying to help this young man to the stairs. I didn't know you were behind me," she said to the other guard.

"You elbowed me in the gut ... hard!" he wheezed.

"And I am so sorry! Why don't you come down the stairs here and I'll get both of you one of my remedies? You'll be good as new before you know it."

Flynn heard the footsteps approaching the stairs. One guard was muttering about Granny being a lot stronger than she looked. "Here we are!" came Granny's sing-song voice. "The kitchen is just off to the left of the foot of the stairs. Be careful now. You two aren't looking well," she chuckled in spite of herself.

The guards started down the stairs and Granny slyly shifted a thin sheet of ice on the steps. The guards' feet went out from under them and they tumbled down the staircase and onto the landing. The guards groaned rubbing a plethora of bumps and bruises.

"What do you two think you are doing?" Flynn shouted. He had come running when he heard the noise. "This isn't a circus act! We are here under direct command of the Karakan!"

Granny rushed down the steps "Oh, don't blame them! It's all my fault! I feel terrible!" she said wringing her hands. "I was afraid something like this might happen. The house just wasn't ready for visitors." She looked apologetically at Flynn.

"Were you able to finish your search?" he asked the groaning men who had managed to get to their feet.

"Yes, it's clear," one answered as he tenderly fingered the large bump on his forehead.

"Please let me make things right," Granny entreated. "I have a remedy that will have you bright-eyed and bushy-tailed in no time at all."

Flynn hesitated. It seemed that wherever that little woman went, trouble followed. It was almost as if she intended to do them harm. But Granny's face was the picture of innocence and he waved the thoughts away.

"I'll just fret all night if you don't let me make it up to you," Granny added spreading on the guilt as thickly as possible.

Flynn looked at Oregg's elderly mother. She was a respected member of the community and she looked harmless. What could an old family remedy hurt? So he agreed and the men followed her into the kitchen.

She poured each of them a glass of cold lemonade. "Now this delicious lemonade is a secret family recipe and this," she said holding up a bottle with red powder in it, "is a cure-all. It soothes cuts, bruises, tummy aches, headaches, arthritis, rashes—"

"We get the idea," Flynn interrupted. Granny started to sprinkle the glasses with the powder. Flynn held up a hand. "None for me, thanks."

"Suit yourself," she replied and stirred the powder into the remaining glasses. "There now. Drink up."

The men sipped the lemonade. "Wow! This is really good," Flynn replied feeling pleasantly surprised. This had turned out to be a good idea after all. The other two nodded their agreement and asked for seconds and thirds.

"I think I'm starting to feel better already," said one.

"You should start to feel the effects pretty quickly," Granny smiled sweetly.

Just then, two guards burst into the kitchen holding Oregg between them. "We've found him, Sir. He was out raking the yard. He must not have seen us come up to the house."

"He looks different," Flynn observed. And he was right. He still had the big red bushy beard, but there was not a single hair on his head. They were all hidden nicely under the skull cap his mother had given him. "I didn't think the councilman was bald," Flynn commented.

"He's not," Granny replied. "My son has a full head of magnificent hair. You've captured the wrong man. This is our gardener, Floregg."

"You don't really expect us to buy that story do you?" Flynn asked skeptically.

"Show 'em, Floregg. Show 'em your weed picking technique," Oregg glared at his mother. She was having fun with this and enjoying the fact that she could pretty much make him do any silly thing she wanted right now. He shook his head and bent down and showed the Elite how he'd pluck little weeds and really tug at the big ones.

"There now," Granny replied. "My son would know nothing about pulling weeds. "The boy hasn't pulled a single weed in his life."

"Well, if he's truly a gardener," Flynn started, "then why is he gardening at night?"

"Oh that's just my son's pride. He likes everyone to think he does the yard work himself. That he's a good old boy, not a high-falutin councilman that has gotten too big for his britches, and is hardly home anymore." Oregg's eyes widened in dismay. Was she trying to give him away? Were these games really worth the risk of getting caught? But, that was his mother.

Flynn looked closely at Oregg. "He looks a lot like Councilman Oregg. A lot. Just without the hair."

"He gets that a lot," Granny replied. "In fact, I think that just might be why my son hired him. If the gardener gets caught cleaning the yard, they might just think it was him."

One of the guards who had drunk the lemonade started to groan as his stomach rumbled loudly. "Uh, Sir, I don't feel well."

"Yeah, agreed," said the other lemonade drinker. "My stomach burns."

Granny nodded. "Oh, that just means it is working. It starts with a slow burn and then works up to a raging inferno, but when the fire dies, you're left fit as a fiddle."

Flynn looked at his suffering men and then back at Oregg and Granny. Her arguments were laughable, but she was so confident. She was either telling the truth, or an expert liar. "When your son returns, tell him to report to the Citadel immediately."

Granny waved to the men as they walked down the path in front of the house. "Now here's a little goodbye present," she muttered to herself and shifted a thin sheet of ice on the path in front of the Elite. One went down taking the rest with him like a row a dominos and it was just their luck that Granny's thorny rose bush was there to break their fall.

"Oh, come back inside and I'll make a poultice out of that cure-all powder," she called.

"No, no. You've helped quite enough," Flynn called back ordering his men to march double time out of Hydra. The Elite scrambled off the premises like a bunch of scared rabbits.

Granny smiled with a wicked glint in her eye. "Until we meet again, boys," she said quietly as she closed the door behind them.

Pulling off the skull cap, Oregg joined her at the door. "They'll be back," he said. "We need to go. Gather up your things, Mother. We need to leave Galvadon for good."

"You're right. We need to leave Hydra for now. But I disagree about leaving Galvadon altogether. Sometimes the best place to hide is out in the open," she said grabbing her duffle bag of disguises. "Besides, my work in Galvadon is not quite finished."

There was a knock at the door. Granny expected to find the Elite asking for more punishment but instead she found Attendant Phrip looking up at her.

"I've come to warn you," started Phrip. "The Karakan is planning to disband the Supreme Council. None of the council is safe."

"How do you know this?" Oregg asked, stepping out from behind the door.

"I think the Karakan has forgotten about me," Phrip replied. "I was in my little room finishing up some things and I overheard him talking with Silvane."

"Well, we'll just have to get to the councilmen before he does," Granny replied.

"And one more thing," Phrip began. "I understand you are sympathetic to the Drek."

"Yes," Granny replied. "I count them as friends and fellow Galvadonians."

"The Karakan has captured them all and placed them in the stocks in the center of town as an example of those that defy him," said Phrip.

"Shame on him!" Granny chided. "Well we most certainly will have to do something about that."

"Take me with you," Phrip pleaded. "I'd like to help if I can." Oregg nodded at his mother and the decision was made.

"Welcome aboard, Phrip!" Granny congratulated. "But hold on to your britches. It's going to be quite a ride before we're through."

CHAPTER 6

Earning Trust

Yondel and Scithe hiked to the base of the mountain that night and then set up camp. Yondel shifted an igloo and crawled in and went to sleep without a word. Scithe made his own arrangements.

The next morning they had hiked halfway up the mountain and had reached the snow before Yondel said anything. "You know I don't like you, right?" she glared at the Terran.

"You've made that abundantly clear," Scithe replied with a sigh.

"Good," she replied and the two walked in silence for a time.

"I think you'd be surprised though," said Scithe.

"Surprised about what?" Yondel asked.

"About me," he replied.

"What could possibly surprise me about you? You're nasty, cruel, and callous."

"Those all mean the same thing," Scithe noted.

"Yes they do. They are all synonyms for Scithe Silvane," Yondel replied.

Scithe just took it as patiently as he could. He knew why she hated him, and he deserved it. If he were Yondel, he would hate him, too. "Did I mention Jonuke and I get along now?"

"Several times, but I still don't believe you. You have connections with the Elite. They could have discovered that information about the Book of Truth," she reasoned.

"But I've been living with him and his family for a while now," he said. "And," he added as an afterthought, "I was dismissed as an Elite. Any connections I had with them are severed."

"Oh, not again. If I say I believe you will you stop telling me the same story over and over again?" she begged.

"It's a deal." Scithe held out his hand to shake on the agreement, but Yondel ignored the gesture. Scithe let his hand drop to his side. "I've said I'm sorry about a hundred times. What's it gonna take for you to forgive me?" Yondel was silent.

"What if I let you throw this snowball at me?" He reached down and packed a handful of snow into a ball. "Would that do it?"

Yondel took the snowball and threw it at him. "Nope. I still don't like you."

"If I'm making that stuff up about Jonuke then how do I know his father, Londor?" Scithe reasoned.

"Everybody knows that," Yondel parried.

"How about his uncle Renden who has been living with him since he was nine?" Scithe asked.

"Again, the Elite have ways of getting that kind of information," sighed Yondel.

"How about the fact that I've been hunting with him in the Darke Forest and he's told me about every plant, animal, and track out there?" Scithe said confidently.

Yondel stopped and looked at him for a moment. "What about the capel weed?"

"Used for sore throats and ear infections," Scithe replied.

"Twinums?" she asked being careful not to give any hints as to whether this was a plant or animal.

"Stay away from those buggers found in shallow standing water," he warned.

"Why?" Yondel challenged.

"Their bite will make you lose all your hair," Scithe answered triumphantly.

Yondel nodded. He had been right both times. She thought for a minute. "The last two were easy, but what about the sap of the almoot tree?" She knew Jonuke would only share that with someone he really trusted.

"Used for camouflage. You blend in with your environment and can only be seen when you move," Scithe replied.

"So the Drek always keep some with them for emergencies?" she tested.

"No, the sap is only good when fresh. Did I pass the exam?" Scithe asked hopefully.

Yondel was having a hard time convincing herself that Scithe was lying about his relationship with Jonuke, but she wasn't ready to believe the truth. "Impressive, but I still can't believe you," she said stubbornly.

"Can't or won't?" Scithe asked.

"Both," she replied folding her arms across her chest.

Scithe stopped walking and stared at Yondel until she was forced to stop as well. "What?" she asked sharply.

"What if I have irrefutable evidence that Jonuke trusts me with his life? Then will you let go of your grudge against me?" Scithe bargained.

Yondel looked Scithe up and down and considered his proposal. It sounded like a safe bet, but he seemed so sure of himself. "What evidence could you possibly have that could prove that?"

"Agree to let bygones be bygones and I will tell you," he offered, tempting her curiosity.

Yondel hesitated. He was very confident of this bit of information he had. What if it truly was irrefutable? Could she really forgive Scithe after all that he had done? "I'll think about it," she said not wanting to make a promise she couldn't keep.

"That's good enough for me." He paused for effect. "Jonuke told me who he is."

Yondel's eyes narrowed. "What do you mean 'told you who he is?'"

"I mean exactly what you think I mean. I know Jonuke is the Vanguard."

"The Vanguard?" Yondel feigned ignorance of the term. If this was some kind of trick, there was no way she was giving up Jonuke's identity to an Elite spy.

"The rightful ruler of Galvadon. I've seen him Energy shift. I even gave him a few pointers on his technique," he added for good measure.

Yondel was reeling with this new information. How could he know that unless Jonuke truly trusted him with his life? He couldn't and she knew it. "I don't understand why he would tell you that. You are the last guy in Galvadon, besides the Karakan himself, who Jonuke would trust with that kind of information."

"I told you I've changed."

"But you were such a jerk," Yondel exerted.

"*Were*, past tense. I'll take it," Scithe replied. At Yondel's scowl he set the teasing aside. "Yes, I was a jerk," he agreed.

"Not just a jerk, but an annoying ruthless bully," she added.

Scithe nodded. "True also."

Then a flood gate opened and Yondel couldn't hold back any longer. "You cheated in the Games, you tormented us on glup duty to no end, Truen almost died from a poison dart and you didn't bat an eye, you confiscated the golden lute and nearly all of Galvadon was destroyed, then you blamed us for it and we were sentenced to death. DEATH!"

"You have to admit you weren't the easiest to get along with either, always calling me Spike and saying I was the last guy on the planet you'd like to be an Elite with," Scithe replied.

"REALLY?!" Yondel shouted. "What part of having us sentenced to death did you not hear?!"

Scithe was immediately contrite. "You're right. You are right about everything, I'm wrong about everything. You're beautiful. I'm ugly. You're kind. I'm mean. You're fair. I'm not. You're considerate. I'm rude. You're smart. I'm dumb. You have integrity. I'm a cheat. I can see why you think I am the scum of the earth."

Yondel couldn't help but snicker at hearing Scithe say all those terrible things about himself, but she quickly recovered. "Just because I laughed doesn't mean I've forgiven you yet."

"Yet? Then we've made some more progress!" he said enthusiastically.

Yondel smiled again against her will. "Oh! You make me so MAD! You are the vilest person I know. How can Jonuke trust you?"

Scithe shrugged. "I don't know. He really shouldn't, based upon my shady past."

"Shady?" she asked with a raised brow.

"Okay, down right despicable, evil, malevolent past life," he corrected.

"That's better," Yondel said with a twinkle in her eye.

"Truce?" Scithe asked tentatively.

Yondel looked at Scithe for a long minute. She couldn't believe she was even considering it. Her granny had been right. She had a lot of pent up anger when it came to Scithe and she almost didn't want to let it go. He deserved all of it, but she also longed for the peace of being free of the grudge. It took a lot of energy to be mad.

Finally, she held out her hand and said, "Truce." The two shook on their agreement. "But if you ever—"

"I won't. Trust me. I don't think I could ever face another round of your wrath again," Scithe said frankly.

"Show me I can trust you and I will," she replied.

By this time the two were at the top of the snow-capped mountain. The ice covered lake glistened in the morning light. Yondel used her gift to part the ice and water and walked down to the bottom of the lake. "Come on down. It's dry as a bone." She kicked the dirt with the toe of her boot.

"If it's alright with you, I'll stay up here," Scithe answered looking uneasily at the walls of water on either side of Yondel. "That much water makes me nervous."

Yondel walked along the lake's bottom until she came to its center. "I found it!" She bent down and picked up a furry looking plant. "It's so soft," she said, petting its fluffy leaves.

Suddenly, the ground cracked open where she removed the plant. "Look out!" Scithe shouted.

Yondel saw the crack snaking toward her and started to walk quickly and then jog toward the edge of the lake. Then there was a loud *snap!* and the crack tripled in size.

"Run!" Scithe yelled. Eyes flashing green, he fought to close the crack, but the entire floor of the lake was breaking up. "What in the *world*?" he exclaimed.

Yondel glanced over her shoulder and saw the crack gaping after her. She tripped and the crack snaked in front of her, swallowing her whole. Yondel was left dangling from the side of the abyss. Without Yondel to hold it back, the ice and water came crashing down.

Scithe dove and caught Yondel's hand. He shifted the rocks beneath their feet into a tower and rocketed them into the air high above the waves that crashed below.

Yondel looked down at the water and then at Scithe. "You saved my life," she said not believing her own words.

"I did promise Granny," Scithe teased. "She trusts me you know."

"Well, and now, so do I," Yondel replied.

CHAPTER 7

M'lai and Iliana

"How are we going to get into Aeris?" Yondel asked looking up at the city. "Not only is it up in the clouds but there are a lot more Elite patrolling Galvadon than before we left. It feels like the mood in Galvadon has changed. It's darker somehow. Do you think my dad made it out safely?"

"Are you kidding? We left him in Granny's hands," Scithe replied.

Yondel chuckled, "You're right. It's the Elite that were assigned to bring my dad in that we should be worried about, right?"

"Speaking as one who has been on the receiving end of your granny's gracious hospitality, I would have to agree with you on that one."

Scithe studied the mountain before them. The Aerisians had built their city atop a steep plateau. "They don't really need guards around their city like the rest of us do. You'd have to really want to get into Aeris to take on this bad boy," he said patting the side of the mountain. He paused for a moment considering his options. "Well, I don't see any other way. We're going to have to do it the old fashioned way."

"You're expecting me to climb that thing?" Yondel asked, supporting the back of her neck with her hand as she strained to see the top of the plateau. "How is that even possible?"

"Like this," Scithe replied as he shifted a rock staircase that extended into the clouds. "That's what I meant by the old-fashioned way."

"Whew! I'll take a staircase any day over dangling from the side of a cliff," Yondel finished as she trudged up the stairs.

*****

Several cloaked figures watched Scithe and Yondel climb the stairs to Aeris. "Should we take them now, General?" one asked.

"No, I'd like to see where they are going first," he replied.

*****

When they got to the top, Yondel was amazed by what she saw. She'd never been to Aeris and had always wondered what the Aerisians had built up here. She'd always envisioned they all lived in cloud dwellings, but now that she thought about it, that wouldn't be very practical. If an unexpected gust of wind blew your house away when you were in the tub or something ... "That would be awkward," she said aloud.

"What would be awkward?" Scithe asked.

Yondel blushed. "Nothing. I was just talking to myself."

Scithe shrugged. "This city is pretty amazing. The Terrans could learn a few things about style from these guys."

Harnessing the power of the wind, the Aerisians had sculpted the plateau into a series of dwellings that were all connected, but still unique. The structures were so detailed, it was as if a master sculptor had molded them out of a fluid medium, not sandstone. The architecture varied, of course, depending upon the skill of the Aerisian that lived there, but the city was uniformly beautiful.

One house was squarely built with faux bricks etched into the outer walls. Another was oval shaped with swirl designs. One looked like an actual seashell from the ocean with all the grooves and points in all the proper places.

"How are we going to find your mom in all this?" Yondel asked.

Just then an Aerisian flew through town with a megaphone to amplify his voice. "It's Tornado Tuesday. Secure your belongings and the cleaning will begin."

Aerisians hurried from their homes clutching breakables and then a team of cleaners sent a series of tornados through the town cleaning every speck of dirt and grime from the homes as they went.

"That's it," Yondel announced. "A public service that cleans your house? I'm moving here."

Scithe scanned the different faces of the people who had gathered to the center of town. He saw a girl he recognized pushing a woman in a wheelchair. "There she is!" he cried.

The Tornado Cleaning Service finished the job as quickly as it began and the Aerisians started back into their homes. Scithe didn't let his mom and sister out of his sight and followed them back to their home. He hesitated at the door.

"What are you waiting for?" Yondel asked.

"I'm nervous. What if she doesn't want to see me?" he asked anxiously.

"She's your mother. She's dying to see you ... Oh, sorry! I didn't mean it that way," Yondel apologized.

Scithe smiled. "I know you didn't. But you do have a point. I have the medicine that will save her life. That has to earn me at least a few brownie points, doesn't it?"

"A *ton* of brownie points," Yondel agreed.

Scithe knocked on the door and Scithe's sister answered the door. "Can I help you?" she asked politely.

"We heard your mom was sick and we brought something that might help," Scithe replied.

"How kind of you," she said opening the door wide with a sweet smile. "Come in." Scithe thought his sister had a kind, trusting way about her and he liked her immediately. The girl showed them into the house and announced, "Mother, there are some people to see you."

Scithe's mother was lying on a couch resting. She sat up and looked at the visitors. "Silvane?" she gasped, her pale complexion turning grey. "How did you find me?" She struggled to sit up.

"No, it's okay. It's me, Scithe," he soothed.

The woman froze and looked into Scithe's eyes for a full minute. "It *is* you!" A single tear rolled down her cheek. "How I have missed you and wondered if you were safe. Come here." She patted the couch next to her and held out her arms. He walked over to her, hugged her, and then sat next to her.

"Let me look at you. You look so much like your father, so handsome and strong." She peered over at her daughter who was hiding behind Yondel. "Iliana, meet your brother, Scithe."

Scithe stood and peered around Yondel. "Hi, Iliana, I'm Scithe and I've always wanted a sister." He offered his hand in greeting.

Shyly she stepped out from behind Yondel and took his hand. "And I've always wanted a brother."

"Well, now," he replied. "It looks like today is turning out to be a rather good day for the both of us."

"Who's your friend, Scithe?" his mother asked indicating Yondel.

"Oh, I almost forgot. This is Yondel," Scithe introduced.

"Pleased to meet you, Yondel. I'm M'lai and this is my daughter Iliana."

Yondel nodded. "Pleased to meet you both. You have a beautiful daughter, M'lai. She looks just like you." Iliana blushed.

"You are so kind. Thank you," M'lai replied. "Please sit down. Both of you. Sit." She indicated two chairs and Iliana sat down next to her mother.

M'lai was looking drawn and tired. Iliana stood and fluffed the pillows on the couch. "Mother you need to rest. It looks like all the wonderful news has really taken it out of you."

Scithe brightened. "Mother, that's just why we've come! Yondel and I have found a cure for your illness. He reached into his knapsack and pulled out the plant.

"Where did you find that?" M'lai asked with astonishment, recognizing the plant immediately. "How did you know I was sick?"

"It's a long story," Scithe replied. "Let's get you well first and then I'll tell you all about it. I promise."

M'lai instructed Iliana on how to prepare the plant by finely chopping its leaves and then pulverizing them with a mortar and pestle. When she finished, M'lai said, "Bring it to me, dearest." Iliana obeyed and M'lai took a small amount of the pulp and placed it under her tongue. Then, she sat back against her pillows and closed her eyes.

Color started to return to her face and her shallow breathing returned to normal. "I haven't seen her look this good for a long time. Thank you," said Iliana.

M'lai looked over at Scithe. "I've wanted to tell you why I left. I didn't want to leave you. I tried to bring you with me."

Scithe smiled compassionately. "I know mother. It's okay. I'm all grown up now and just glad I have you back in my life."

"And your father?" she asked, voice trembling.

"I never wanted for anything," Scithe replied. What could he say? Silvane was far from the ideal father.

M'lai read between the lines. "I'm so sorry, son. I'm so glad you found me. Now we can be a family again." His mother sat up. "You know what? I'm starting to feel better already."

Just then Silvane threw open the front door and walked into the room. "Well, well, well. It's a family reunion! M'lai, you've been hiding here all these years right in front of my face. Who knew? And all I had to do was follow these two," he pointed to Scithe and Yondel, "and they led me right to you."

Silvane's eyes came to rest on Iliana. With that shock of thick dark hair and her uncanny resemblance to her mother, he quickly put the pieces together. "A daughter?" He was quiet for a moment. Scithe thought he saw a brief emotion in his eyes but his father quickly covered it up.

Scithe stepped between Silvane and his mother. "They're not your family anymore, Silvane. You don't deserve them."

Silvane's countenance darkened. "How dare you address me that way," he breathed. "Guards!" he called and two guards came through the door. "The Karakan will be interested in dealing with these traitors personally. Take them all back to the Citadel."

Scithe wasn't about to let Silvane take his mother from him again. He shifted the wall so it knocked Silvane and his men down and then turned to Yondel. "Please, get my family out of here. I'll hold the Elite off."

"But—" M'lai started.

"All I care about is you and Iliana. I need to know you are both safe," he said. Then to Yondel, "Promise me you'll help them."

"I promise," she replied solemnly and the three girls disappeared through the gaping hole in the wall.

"Argh!" Silvane yelled scrambling to his feet and seeing most of his prisoners had escaped. "Go after them!" he ordered the dazed guards who rushed through the opening in the wall. Silvane turned on Scithe. "You are a traitor and a disgrace. I am repulsed at the thought that we are related."

"Funny," Scithe replied. "I was just about to say the same thing about you. How could you treat my mother the way you did?"

"She is my wife and no concern of yours."

"*Was* you wife, but she *is* my mother and it is very much my concern. The only thing she ever did wrong was to marry you."

"Oh, so you think you can wound me with your words, son?"

"I have no father, remember?" Scithe shot back.

"Enough! You are a traitor to Galvadon—"

"Maybe to the Karakan but not Galvadon," Scithe interrupted. "You are the only one here who has betrayed Galvadon."

Enraged, Silvane shifted a sandstone hand from the ground that grabbed Scithe tightly. "You've disrespected me long enough," Silvane raged.

"That's ... assuming ...," Scithe gasped as the hand tightened, squeezing the air from his lungs, "I respected ... you in the ... first place." And then he lost consciousness.

*****

"Mother, are you well enough to travel?" Iliana asked as the three emerged from the house.

"The medicine works quickly once it's in the system, my love. I'm as good as new," M'lai replied.

Yondel got them to the border of Aeris before the guards caught up with them. "Surrender immediately and your punishment may be lessened."

"Ha!" Yondel scoffed. "Not likely."

"Have it your way," the Aerisian shrugged. He sent a powerful gust of wind that knocked the three girls off their feet.

"Are you alright, M'lai?" Yondel asked with concern.

"Don't worry about me. I'm fine," M'lai replied. "I'm sorry I can't be of more help. Our abilities are very limited."

"You two stay behind me. I can take these guys." Yondel replied as her gaze came to rest on an old stone well. Yondel's eyes glowed blue as she summoned the water from the well and used it to freeze the guards into a solid block of ice. "That was easy," she said brushing her hands together as a gesture of a job well done.

"Let's get you out of here," Yondel said to M'lai. "I hate to say it, but the Darke Forest is probably safer for you than Galvadon right now. I have a Drek friend that is ... out of town right now. You can use his place until he gets back. Look! You can see it from here." She pointed to Jonuke's home on the edge of the lake. "See it?" M'lai nodded. "We—"

Yondel was interrupted by a high pitched whistling sound. She glanced over her shoulder at the frozen Elite who had somehow managed to make several small holes in the ice by focusing jet streams of air on the obstacle. These holes were the source of the ear-piercing whistling.

Yondel had to cover her ears protectively and watched helplessly as the guards broke through the ice. Before she could react, she was caught in a whirlwind, spinning round and round. She was so dizzy she couldn't think straight. Suddenly, Yondel fell to the ground and everything seemed to reel to and fro as she got her bearings. She was so confused, she thought she saw M'lai and Iliana Wind shifting.

Yondel got to her feet. She wasn't confused after all. They *were* Wind shifting but the Elite were far more skilled than they and the girls were in trouble. Yondel shifted a wall of ice around the guards. "Run!" she called out. She shifted an ice slide from the side of the plateau all the way to the ground. "Go down it! Now!" she yelled as the Elite broke through the ice wall and came after them.

"We can't leave without you, Yondel," Iliana pleaded.

"I promised Scithe," Yondel said calmly. "Please go … for him. I'll hold them off."

Yondel watched as Scithe's loved ones made it safely down the slide and ran into the forest. She sighed her relief and then turned to face the guards. "Bring it on, boys. Bring-it-on."

CHAPTER 8

Right Under Their Noses

Oregg had easily convinced Falnor that the tide had turned in Galvadon, but the Pyrosian was having difficulty leaving his new wife. "The less she knows, the better," Oregg reasoned. "She will be questioned when you are found missing. You will be able to see her again as soon as things quiet down." Ultimately, Falnor was persuaded to leave Pyros.

Fantisma had surprised everyone by being packed and ready to go when Granny came to the door. Granny had left Oregg, Falnor and Phrip in the tunnels, but before she could leave with Fantisma, Flynn showed up with his squad. Granny directed Fantisma to the location of the tunnel and promised to distract the Elite while the councilwoman made her escape.

Opening her duffle of disguises, Granny pulled out some ragged clothing and put on a white frumpy-looking wig. She glued on two thick bushy eyebrows and a hairy wart on her nose. When the Elite demanded entry, she again let them into the house and explained that Fantisma had gone for an evening stroll.

"What is it with these councilmen and walks?" one of the guards asked.

"Who are you?" Flynn demanded.

"Why I'm the cleaning lady," Granny replied.

His eyes narrowed as he studied Granny. "Have we met before?"

Granny smiled, revealing what appeared to be missing teeth, but she had just blackened them moments before. "I wish!" she replied in a thick southern accent. "Better late than never, though" She reached out to tickle Flynn's chin, but he dodged her reaching fingers. "Nope," she continued, "I woulda 'membered meetin' a handsome feller like yerself." She winked at him and lifted her eyebrows up and down suggestively.

Is she flirting with me? Flynn grimaced at the thought. *She has to be more than twice my age, no twice my mother's age!* "Ma'am, we'll need to search the house," he said.

"I wouldn't have it any other way, handsome," Granny winked again. Flynn shivered and walked in to Fantisma's home.

The three councilmen waiting in the tunnel winced at the crashes and hollers they heard coming from the house. "Is she okay in there?" Fantisma asked.

"Oh, she's fine," Oregg replied.

"I'm sure glad Edween is on our side," Falnor smiled. A few minutes later they watched the Elite flee the house. Granny joined the refugees in the tunnel.

"Three of you are safe and sound. Now one to go," she said.

Rottmoth's ostentatious granite castle, complete with turrets and green fluttering flags, was easy to find. The council knew Rottmoth would be a hard sell, so they decided that it was best if they all approached the doorway together.

"Rottmoth, you need to come with us. The Karakan has ordered our arrest," Oregg started.

"I don't believe you," Rottmoth said trying to close the door, but Oregg's foot was preventing him.

"What do we have to gain by fabricating such a story?" Falnor asked.

"You and Oregg haven't been the most loyal supporters of the Karakan and Fantisma—she's just confused," Rottmoth replied.

"You only think I'm flakey because I want you to think that," Fantisma replied. "What they are saying is the truth. Come with us now for your own safety."

They were all taken aback by Fantisma's lucidity. "No," Rottmoth said, "I can't believe the Karakan would turn on me. He knows I support him," he concluded.

"Have it your way," Oregg replied. The small group was forced to leave Rottmoth to fend for himself. Just as they were leaving the grounds they nearly ran into Flynn and his bedraggled squad.

"Quickly, hide behind the wall," Granny whispered. They watched as Flynn knocked on the door and demanded entry. When Rottmoth answered the door, Flynn seemed almost surprised that he had found a councilman at home. "The Karakan has asked to speak with you," Flynn explained.

Rottmoth looked at the squad of Elite standing behind him. "Since when does it take an entire Elite squad to request a meeting with a member of the Supreme Council?"

"They are only here to prevent any trouble," Flynn replied.

"Trouble?" Rottmoth repeated. He had a sinking feeling in his stomach as he realized what his fellow councilmembers had told him was true.

"Men, escort Councilman Rottmoth to the Citadel," Flynn ordered. His fellow councilmen watched from behind the wall as Rottmoth's hands were tied behind his back and he was taken from his home.

"How are we going to help him now?" Falnor asked.

"Help him?" Oregg asked. "We tried and he wouldn't listen. Maybe all that kissing up he did to the Karakan will save him."

"We all have been blinded at one time or another by the Karakan's flattery," Phrip started.

"Not I," said Granny.

"Well, almost everyone then. Rottmoth is one of our own and deserves a second chance, just like we've been given," Phrip finished.

"Alright," Granny agreed. "We'll give it one more try. I've got an idea." She pulled out her bag of disguises and handed them all something to put on, except for Falnor. "Falnor, you will sneak around to the other side and wait for our distraction. Then grab Rottmoth and meet us in the tunnels. Falnor nodded and disappeared in the darkness.

Oregg held up the disguise his mother had given him. "But these are women's clothes," he complained.

"All the better, dear. Go big or go home," Granny quipped.

"But I have a beard! I can hardly pass for a woman," Oregg reasoned.

"I passed you off as a gardener when the Elite clearly recognized you, didn't I?" Granny reminded him.

"True," Oregg replied.

"Then, trust me son. Now get dressed and follow my lead." Phrip and the others did as they were told. Granny wore a dark brown wig with a long braid that hung down her back and Fantisma had a long black wig with straight hair. Fantisma and her strange-looking friends followed Granny as she chased down the Elite, waving her arms wildly.

"Excuse me!" she called out trying to get their attention. "Excuse me. Are you fellows Elite? Could you help us please? We were traveling with a cart full of our best produce in order to get it to the market first thing in the morning when our wheel fell off."

"Ma'am we are on urgent business for the Karakan," Flynn replied.

"But we've been traveling all night from the outer most part of the city. Please," she begged.

Flynn looked at what he thought to be a group of women. "Where's the cart?" he asked looking at the motley crew. Fantisma and Granny looked fairly normal but Phrip wore a short blonde wig and was the ugliest girl he'd ever seen.

Phrip giggled and flirted with the nearest guard. "You look so strong," Phrip said in a high squeaky voice.

He waved and winked at the guard who looked alarmed by the ugly girl's attention and quickly stepped away.

"Oh, the cart is back there a mile or so," Granny replied pointing behind them.

"We don't have time for—" Flynn did a double take when his eyes came to Oregg. The councilman was wearing a full skirt and a curly red wig that matched his beard. Flynn's eyes narrowed. "Wait a minute!"

"Oh, that's Oreggina. Don't mention the beard, dear," Granny whispered to Flynn. "She's very self-conscious about it."

"But isn't that—?" Then he looked more closely at Granny. "And aren't you—?"

"Absolutely not! We've never met, young man!" she shrieked as she slapped Flynn across the face. Granny had everyone's attention now and Falnor took his opportunity to whisk Rottmoth to the tunnel.

"How dare you talk to me with such familiarity? I'm not that kind of girl!" She glanced over to make sure Falnor was safely away. "Come on, girls! We'll find someone else to help us."

The Elite stared after the strange women for a full minute before recovering from the experience. "Sir, Councilman Rottmoth is gone!" one of the guards shouted.

"Gone?!" Flynn yelled. They searched the surrounding area but the prisoner was long gone. "It was a setup,"

Flynn said quietly. "And it was the same woman every time! After them!" But Granny and her little band of refugees had vanished without a trace.

*****

"Enter!" the Karakan called. Flynn walked into the old council room. The Karakan had requested he meet him there when he learned of his failure to bring in the members of the Supreme Council.

The Karakan turned to the mural of the Darke Forest painted on the wall. "You see this painting? I've concluded this is the best place for people who have disappointed me. Do you remember Scithe Silvane? Of course you do. It was his bad luck that brought you onto the Elite, wasn't it? Well, as it turns out, he joined forces with Yondel of Oregg and was stirring up trouble in Aeris.

"Fortunately, I have one competent Elite. Silvane brought them in and now they are here. Do you see them? They are running from some creature in the forest. It's really quite entertaining." He watched them fighting a gnarly-looking beast for a time almost forgetting Flynn was in the room.

"So, I hear you have failed me not one but four times, tonight," the Karakan said calmly.

Too calmly, Flynn thought. "Yes, Sir," Flynn hung his head in shame. He was definitely not getting a promotion. "They knew we were coming."

"Even so, I would think with a squad of Elite you could accomplish the simple task of gathering up the Supreme Council," said the Karakan angrily.

"But they had disguises," reasoned Flynn.

"Disguises?" the Karakan scoffed. "That is the best excuse you have to offer? No, I've had enough of disappointment, Flynn."

The Karakan waved his paintbrush at the Aerisian who disappeared and became part of the painting. The Karakan walked over to the mural "Ah! There you are, Flynn. Now, I wouldn't want you to get bored or lonely so here is a friend to keep you company. The Karakan painted a screecher just above Flynn and laughed as he watched the Aerisian run through the trees, trying to escape. "I feel better already," sighed the Karakan.

Silvane walked into the room and watched Flynn for a time. "It's time Silvane," said the Karakan as he pulled out the Master's Blade. First Galvadon, and then the remaining kingdoms."

*****

The Karakan had left Galvadon to go a conquering so he didn't see that not a single Drek was left in the stocks the next morning. All that remained of them was the sign that used to read "Traitors to the Crown." But now said "The Vanguard Has Returned." Granny couldn't resist leaving behind that final finishing touch.

CHAPTER 9

Taeliah's Secret

Taeliah, Truen and Valent hid behind a rock and watched a leathery skinned animal that was lying in front of the entrance to the cave. Similar to an elephant-sized horny toad, its body was stout and round, and spikes covered its back.

"It's a carlin," Taeliah declared.

"How do you know that?" Truen asked.

"Thael drew a pretty good likeness of it. See?" she said pointing at a crudely drawn circle with two eyeballs and small lines jutting out all over it. There was an arrow pointing to the picture with the word "carlin" next to it.

"I have to say I am developing a deep respect for this Thael guy," Valent said. "He was a great explorer and an artist. How many elves can say that?"

Truen laughed. "I'll say. Anyone that could get past that thing over there must be one awesome dude."

The carlin lifted its head in their direction, and its tongue shot out "smelling" the air. After heaving its bulk up on four short, skinny legs, it wiggled toward them, keeping close to the ground.

"I think it knows we are here," Valent whispered stating the obvious.

"Quick! Under this!" Taeliah yanked a glittering cloak from her knapsack and spread it over the three of them. "He won't be able to see us if we remain completely still.

"An invisibility cloak?" Truen whispered.

"Awesome, right?" Valent replied.

"Not my first thought," murmured Truen. "This could have been helpful with the say, twenty-nine other beasts we've come across."

"Shh!" Taeliah whispered. "It's not soundproof!"

The animal's tongue shot out again searching the air for what its eyes could not see. Climbing atop the rock, the carlin looked directly at the huddled trio but saw nothing. Satisfied, it climbed off the rock and started back to its place in the sun.

"We have to get to the cave before it blocks it again," said Taeliah. "Move quickly, but stay under the cloak."

"No problem," Truen grumbled as they tiptoed awkwardly toward the cave.

It quickly became apparent that the carlin would reach the cave before stumbling trio. Taeliah wasn't about to let that happen. She threw off the cloak and shouted, "Run for the cave. I'll distract it!" The carlin's head snapped around spying its prey. Hissing menacingly it scuttled toward them.

"Are you kidding?" Neither Truen nor Valent was willing to leave this girl to fight this battle alone.

"You said you'd listen back there in the jungle. Trust me, and go!" she said as she pulled out her fighting staff and drove the carlin back. Taeliah was a skilled fighter and handled herself well. "Go!" she yelled again and the boys and made for the cave. They watched as Taeliah darted and dodged, struck and parried in staff to claw combat until the carlin realized the skinny elf wasn't worth the fight and scuttled away. Taeliah swaggered into the cave, her face glowing after her well-earned victory.

"I have to say, you were a blur of awesomeness," Truen commented.

Valent nodded his agreement. "You were amazing, Taeliah. Where did you learn to fight like that?"

"When you are your father's only daughter you learn a lot of things," she replied. The three of them walked deeper into the cave. "So let's have a look at what's in here."

Just then Taeliah groaned and doubled over in pain. "Taeliah!" Valent shouted as he and Truen rushed over to help her sit down. "What's wrong? Were you injured by the carlin? I knew I shouldn't have let you fight that battle alone!" he exclaimed.

Taeliah took a moment to catch her breath. "No, I'm fine really," she said getting to her feet. "The carlin didn't touch me. I'm just tired. It's been a long journey."

As Valent helped her up, he noticed the thick brown skin that he'd seen on her arm had spread to her neck. He hadn't said anything before but he was getting concerned. "Taeliah, your neck ...." he said quietly so she wouldn't be embarrassed in front of Truen.

She reached up and felt the dry cracking skin and covered it up with her hair. "Oh, that," she said nervously. "All this exposure to the sun and wind is really hard on a girl's skin. I'll be fine once we get back home. Something about Taeliah's manner told Valent that she wasn't telling the whole truth, but he wasn't going to push her to share something she wasn't ready to share.

They explored the cave and found it to be very average-looking and worst of all, empty. "Thael's notes say this is the place we are looking for. I don't get it," Taeliah said. She took the old wish stone out of her bag and noticed it had started to glow.

As they traveled deeper into the cave it glowed brighter until they came to a dead end. Taeliah moved it closer to the wall, and a single wish stone appeared. "I found one!" she said as she moved the stone over the wall's surface. There was a flash of color and the cave lit up with a rainbow of gems embedded in the walls.

"Wish stones," Valent said, eyes bright with wonder.

Taeliah ran her hand over them and a voice echoed, "Only the true in heart may obtain a wish stone." And suddenly, Truen, Valent and Taeliah disappeared.

Truen found himself in a place he knew very well, Hej's melon patch. As if he was on automatic pilot he relived the entire experience of pilfering some melons and lava boarding though town until he got back to his house with them. He faced Falnor and Hej for the second time and the results were the same. He saw the gardener walking away frustrated and angry when Falnor wouldn't believe the truth about Truen's thievery. Then his surroundings froze.

"What should you have done differently?" the cave voice echoed.

"What do you mean?" Truen asked.

"At the time, you were only concerned with getting what you wanted, no matter the cost. Is that still all that matters to you?"

Truen didn't like this. He felt uncomfortable watching the effects of his stealing. What had seemed like just a little fun caused hours of cleanup, not to mention the fact the Hej was blamed and had to pay for part of it. It had been wrong and it didn't sit well with him. He felt that he had changed since that day.

"No, it's not all that matters," Truen replied. "I hurt other people. I shouldn't have taken the melons in the first place and I should have admitted my mistake instead of letting Hej take the blame." Suddenly, he was back in the cave, all of them were back in the cave.

"That was strange," Valent said. "I was reliving a memory of a war council when I didn't have the courage to stand up for what was right. Once I admitted I would do things differently, I ended up back here."

"Same thing happened to me," said Taeliah. "But for me it was about sacrificing my time to help others." Truen told them about his experience in the melon patch.

"That is correct," the voice echoed. "You have qualified for a wish stone. Wish wisely."

Taeliah went to the wall and took a stone. It glittered and sparkled in her hand. She put the old wish stone in its place and it immediately grew bright again.

"You know a spare would have saved a lot of hassle," Truen reasoned. "Do you think we qualified for one stone total or one stone each?" he asked. He went to the wall and tried to pull one out, but it didn't budge.

"It looks like one stone total," Valent observed.

Suddenly, Taeliah swooned and Valent caught her just before she hit the ground. "What's wrong, Taeliah?" he said shaking her gently, but she was unresponsive. "Do you think it was the wish stone that did this to her?" he asked Truen.

"I don't know but look at her arms," said Truen. Valent pulled up her sleeve and saw the brown cracked skin was on both arms. "Look it's on her neck, too."

The boys both saw that her skin was changing before their eyes. "The wish stone didn't do this," Valent concluded. "I noticed one of her arms looked like this before we went into the jungle and then again when we first came into the cave."

"It looks like tree bark," Truen noted.

"Wait," Valent said. "She said Thael wished her people could live to the age of a tree. She also said that all the wishes came with consequences but never told us what the consequence of that wish was."

"Are you saying that she is literally changing into a tree before our eyes?" Truen asked. Valent nodded solemnly. "Then let's wish her back to normal. We have a wish stone now."

"No," Valent shook his head and tucked the wish stone away. "She said all the wishes had terrible consequences. We can't risk it. We need to get her home. Her father Raef will know what to do."

"But what if it's too late by the time we get back?" Truen asked. "How are we going to get her there in time?"

"Taeliah told me the vrag can travel quickly." Valent picked up Taeliah, cradling her in his arms. "Let's go."

When the boys got back to the vrag, the animal took one look at the condition of his beloved owner and snarled threateningly at Valent. "Woah, boy. I didn't do it."

He turned and snarled at Truen. "Me either," he said holding his hands up in surrender.

"We need to get her home, boy," Valent explained. "Can you take us back to the village?" The vrag whined and looked anxious to go.

Valent secured Taeliah to the saddle and the boys carefully positioned themselves around the spikes on the vrag's back. No sooner had the boys climbed aboard, than the vrag was off in a flash. Truen and Valent held onto the horns for dear life as they sped, nearly at the speed of light, back to the elfin village.

*****

When they arrived back at the village, it appeared that it had been abandoned. The houses were dark and there was not an elf in sight. "Where is everyone?" Truen asked. The vrag snorted and whined and led them to a tree near the spring.

"You don't suppose—" Valent started.

"That they all turned to trees?" Truen finished. Upon closer observation, they could see that their theory had been correct. They could just make out the outlines of Raef's face in the bark of the tree's trunk.

Valent took Taeliah down from the saddle and placed her near the spring. "We need to figure out how to change them back," he said. He took the wish stone from his pocket and embedded it in the rock in the spring. Immediately the rock enveloped the stone like an old friend. "It's working," he said.

The wish stone glowed a bright magenta, changing the color of the water. "We need to help her drink the water," he said. He placed Taeliah's feet, which had begun to look more like roots than feet, into the water. The boys watched as the glowing water traveled up through her toes, to her legs and trunk, up through her branch-like arms and hands, and to her head and the very ends of her leaf-like hair.

Taeliah began to revive. She sat up and looked at the condition of her body and gasped. "Oh, no! It's begun!"

"It's alright," Valent reassured her. "We put the stone back. It will change you back."

"No, it won't," she said shaking her head. "Where's my father?" But even as she asked the question her eyes came to rest on the tree that was Raef. "It's too late! He's the only one that knows how to change us back! All is lost!" Just then her legs fused together into a solid trunk.

"No!" said Valent. "There has to be a way. Use the wish stone! You have nothing to lose anymore."

"I could lose you," she said sadly.

"And I won't lose you," Valent replied passionately. Then an idea came to him. "Use the healing song that only makes the flowers in your garden wilt. Maybe it will revive your father long enough to help you."

Nodding hopefully, Taeliah began to sing:

Wishing stone, wishing stone,
Hear my plea and grant this true desire to me.
Let him awake from his deep slumber.
Make my father strong once more.

Valent filled his cupped hands with water and poured it on the tree's roots. Slowly, Raef's eyes opened and he looked down at his daughter. "Taeliah!" he barked, his voice rough from lack of use.

"Father!" she cried.

"My time is short. I must transfer the Knowing to you before my life is over," he said deliberately. "I will rely on the power of the wish stone ... to give me the strength to see the process through." He slowly bent over and covered the wish stone with a limb. "You must join your hand with mine, Taeliah. Boys, would you help my daughter?"

Valent and Truen lifted Taeliah to the wish stone. She had become rigid and heavy. Valent helped her lift her limb to the wish stone. This time Raef began to sing:

Wishing stone, wishing stone,
Hear my plea and grant this true desire to me.
Take this Knowing from generations before
And grant this wisdom to her e'er more

Light traveled from the center of Raef's trunk through the wishing stone and into Taeliah. Then her father grew silent and his face disappeared into the bark. There was no evidence that the tree had ever been anything but a tree.

Taeliah slowly regained her strength and stood on her own. Her limbs became arms and legs once more and the bark fell away from her skin. Valent took her in his arms and held her close. "I thought I lost you."

"It will take a lot more than turning into a tree to pry me away from your side," Taeliah smiled.

Valent looked at the tree that was once Raef. "I'm so sorry about your father," he said tenderly. "I guess we got here too late."

She smiled back at him. "You got me here just in time." Taeliah placed her hands on the wish stone and closed her eyes. "You see the secret is to wish from the heart." The wish stone began to glow brightly changing the water to a reddish-purple.

The water altered its course and flowed in a stream up above the trees and then exploded into a thousand raindrops. Raef's shape changed back into human form and the bark fell away. One by one all of the trees changed back into elves. They smiled and hugged one another at the happy reunion.

Raef hugged his daughter and swung her around. "You did it, honey!"

"We did it," she corrected indicating her faithful companions.

"Thank you both for saving my people," said Raef gratefully. "Your debt is repaid and then some. We are better off now than if you had not come at all."

"Check your fire power, Truen. You too, Wolfie," Taeliah teased playfully.

Truen ignited fire underneath each of his feet and he shot up into the air. "It's back! And I can fly!" he exclaimed doing a somersault and returning to the ground. Valent changed into a wolf and back and fire shot from his fingertips. He was more than startled.

Taeliah chuckled. "I wished that all would be restored to its proper place and then some," she said to

Truen and then to Valent, "Your dad was a fire shifter, and now, so are you." Both boys grinned excitedly and thanked Taeliah.

"I hate to break up the party, but my mother will be worried," said Truen. "I need to get back to Galvadon."

"And so will my grandfather," Valent added.

"There is something I must tell you," started Raef. "Galvadon has changed since you left. The Karakan has lengthened the reach of his rule. We have seen many of the kingdoms fall. If we had not been trees, I fear our people would have been taken as well."

"What about Haldan?" Valent asked.

"I'm sorry," Raef replied. "We saw the Elite marching them toward Galvadon."

"Then we must *all* go back to Galvadon," said Taeliah solemnly.

CHAPTER 10

Jealous Much?

Truen didn't recognize the Galvadon he came home to. To say it had changed was an understatement. The four cities: Aeris, Terra, Hydra, and Pyros had been completely abandoned. Instead, the people were living in the center of Galvadon in tall grey tenements with a great wall, a prison wall, surrounding them. The buildings were separated into groups and Truen soon learned why.

The most surprising sight was that Galvadon no longer was a home for just Elementals. Giants lumbered across the city, working to build more tenements under the direction of the dwarves. The wolves from Haldan were strapped to a sled and used to hall the materials for the buildings. Gnomes were scurrying about delivering clothing. The Elementals were busy with menial tasks like gardening, laundry, cooking, and landscaping—work that had previously assigned only to the Drek. The chores would have been so much easier to complete with their gifts. Why weren't they using them?

"It so different from what we saw when we were last here," Taeliah observed.

"I'm really worried about my mom," said Truen.

"You must go find her," Valent offered his hand to his brother in parting. "Taeliah and I will do what we can to help my people. Until we meet again, brother." Truen took his hand and Valent pulled his younger brother into a hug. "It'll be okay," Valent reassured. Truen nodded and the three parted company.

The walls of the city were heavily patrolled by the Elite. Truen waited for his opportunity and then used his new fire blasters to fly over the wall and into the city. Elite were stationed throughout the city overseeing the labor of the people. He was going to have to keep a low profile to avoid being noticed by the guards. When he left Galvadon, he became a fugitive from the law.

All the tenements looked the same, dull and hopeless, and that was also the feeling of the city. The Elementals had been conquered and forced from their homes. The people trudged to complete their tasks, hunched over and defeated. Why didn't they fight back? He knew something terrible had happened here and he was anxious to find out what.

Truen located the Pyrosian tenements and saw his mother through one of the windows. He climbed the stairs to her apartment and knocked on the door. When his mother answered the door, he noticed the lines of worry etched in her face. "Truen? You're alive?" she gasped looking into the hallway to make sure he hadn't been seen. "Come in! Quickly." She closed the door behind him and then hugged him tightly. "We must be very careful. You are wanted for treason."

The two of them sat down and his mother took his hands in her own. "How I've missed you! Where have you been?"

Truen told her of his adventures and of his success in finding the wish stone. She gasped and sighed at the peril he had faced and asked him many questions. After he had answered them all, it was Truen's turn to ask a few questions. "The Karakan has taken over Galvadon and the surrounding lands? How?" he asked.

"The Karakan came into the cities with his Elite guard and demanded that we bow to him as Supreme Ruler of Galvadon. This did not sit well with the Elementals and they resisted, but the Karakan expected that. He had a powerful sword in his possession, a Master's Blade. The Pyrosians tried to use Fire against him, but anything they sent at him was repelled and turned back on them. The Karakan and his sword was stronger than anyone—stronger than all of them combined. They soon learned that no one, no matter how strong their Fire shifting abilities could defeat him. The other cities learned the same thing."

"What about Falnor? Where is he?" Truen asked.

"The Karakan's first act was to disband the Council, but when they came looking for Falnor, he had already been warned, and he escaped. Knowing I would be questioned, which I was, he didn't tell me where he was going. I was worried at first, but could answer truthfully that I didn't know where he was. The Council is wanted for treason, so he is in hiding now, but he checks in on me frequently."

"The Elementals have become slaves. Why don't they fight back?" Truen asked.

"Shifting is forbidden unless it is specifically commissioned for an assignment," his mother explained. Truen couldn't believe he was living in a Galvadon without Element shifting.

"You said the councilmen are on the run. What about Hydra?" he asked.

Truen's mother knew he was concerned about Yondel. "I'm so sorry, dearest. I haven't seen Yondel since the Karakan took over." Truen looked as if he had been punched in the stomach.

"It is said," his mother continued, "that the Karakan has a special prison in the Citadel for those that fight against him. All the leaders of the kingdoms are kept there."

"That's where she is," Truen replied. "I have to go find her."

"The Citadel is forbidden to all but the Elite. Any who enter unbidden ..." her voice trembled, "never come out." She started to sob. "Don't go Truen! I can't lose you again. You're my only son. I don't think I will recover from another broken heart."

Truen held her hand and lifted her chin so he was looking into her teary eyes. "I will stay if you ask me to," he said tenderly.

"Why did you have to say that?" she chuckled in spite of herself. "You know I can't ask that of you when Yondel is missing. Please fix this, Truen. Bring Yondel back."

"I will, Mother." He hugged her and said, "And I promise you that I will always find my way back home."

Truen crept through the city to the Citadel. Checking to make sure he hadn't been seen he opened the front door and tiptoed down the hallway. He heard voices and followed them to the old council room. Waiting until two guards emerged, he slid in through the door before it closed completely. The room was dark and empty and there were clearly no prisoners here.

He looked around the room. He'd lost count of how many times he'd been in here for disciplinary councils. It was really strange being in here without the council. The great tree still stood at the room's center. The council table was there surrounded by empty chairs, and a mural of the Darke Forest covered one of the walls.

Something about the painting caught his eye, and he walked over to it to have a closer look. There were people in the painting standing next to a stone structure. He was sure they hadn't been there the last time he had seen this painting. It had always just been a forest, no people. One person in particular looked familiar ....

"Yondel?" he said aloud. Yondel looked around for the source of the voice she had just heard. But didn't seem to be able to see Truen standing there.

"Yondel! It's me, Truen!" he said urgently. How was he going to get her out of a painting? He reached out to touch her image and his hand changed into a two dimensional painted image. He tried to withdraw it but he couldn't. He struggled as he felt himself being pulled into the painting, but it was no use.

As Truen disappeared into the painting, two figures stepped out from the shadows in the corner of the room. "You said the trouble-making Pyrosian was back in Galvadon and that he would come for his Hydran friend," the Karakan said to Silvane. "Well done, Silvane, well done. I see your generalship was well-earned.

The two left the room without a backward glance.

*****

As Truen entered the painting, he saw that he was no longer three dimensional. He was a two dimensional picture of himself. He looked at his arms and hands, and yep, they were painted on. His entire body was made of paint. He saw that he was in the painting of the Darke Forest and it was depicted perfectly down to the smallest detail. He recognized the building he'd seen Yondel standing next to, but she was nowhere in sight. He decided to check inside the building.

Inside the rock fort that Scithe had built for their protection, Scithe and Yondel were talking quietly. Althhough some time had passed, he was still worried about the safety of his mother and his sister.

"Are you sure the Elite didn't see her?" he asked.

"I'm absolutely sure. I saw them running into the Darke Forest. They'll be safe in Jonuke's house. And, remember, she has your sister. I'm sure they're just fine. As soon as we find a way out of here, we'll go get them."

"I hope your right." Scithe smiled thankfully at his friend. "Thanks, Yondel, for talking to me about this. Again. And thank you for making sure they got out of Galvadon safely. You are a true friend."

"Anytime," she replied and leaned over to give him a brotherly hug. "But I still don't get how she was able to shift the Wind like that—"

And that was the moment Truen walked in. "What is going on here?!" he demanded staring in disbelief at Yondel in Scithe's arms.

Yondel shot to her feet. "Truen? How did you find us? Do you know how to get out of here?"

Truen's face was red with fury. All he could see was his mortal enemy making his move on his girl, and he couldn't hear a word Yondel said. "You!" he said pointing to Scithe. "How dare you?! How dare you even look at her?! You shouldn't even be in the same room together!" A fireball ignited in his hand and he hurled it at Scithe who luckily dodged out of the way.

Yondel realized that Truen had been away from Galvadon. He didn't know that Scithe had changed, that he was one of them now. "Stop, Truen!" she shouted as Truen sent a volley of fireballs at Scithe who had shifted a stone wall between them for protection. The wall was turning red from the heat and Scithe had to back up to avoid being roasted.

"Come out and fight me, coward!" Truen demanded.

"Truen, Scithe's changed," Yondel said stepping in front of her Pyrosian friend, but he just stepped around her and continued to pelt Scithe's wall with fireballs.

"Okay, I tried reason and that isn't working," she said calmly. Yondel walked over to a pitcher of water, picked it up, and threw it at Truen. Her eyes flashed blue and she froze Truen solid.

Scithe peeked out from behind the barricade, "Is it safe to come out now?" he called out to Yondel, but she shook her head and signaled him to stay behind the wall.

"Now that you've cooled off a bit, Truen," she chuckled at her pun. "We can have a calm, reasonable discussion. Are you ready for that? Or do you need a few more minutes to get ahold of yourself?"

Truen melted the ice around his lips. "I need a few more minutes," he said. And then after a short pause asked, "Why were you hugging him? Has your memory been wiped or something?"

"He's changed, Truen. Even Jonuke likes him," she reasoned.

"So you admit that you like him?" asked Truen. "Now I know your mind has been altered. There's no way Jonuke likes that guy."

Yondel laughed. "I had a hard time believing it, too, but you really can trust him. If he was on the Karakan's team, why would he be in here with us?"

"He could be a spy," Truen suggested.

"He could, but he's not," she replied. "He knows Jonuke is the Vanguard."

"How could he know that?" Truen asked suspiciously.

"Jonuke told him," Yondel answered. She explained about how Scithe and Jonuke had quested for the Master's Blade together. She went on to tell him how she and Scithe had gone after a medicinal plant for Scithe's mother and how they had been captured by the Elite and then painted into the mural.

"I still think it could all be a rouse," Truen's lips replied stubbornly.

"You're just going to have to trust me, Truen. He's okay," she finished.

"But you still haven't explained why you were letting him hug you like that. You two looked pretty chummy," Truen accused.

"We are chummy, but not in the way you're thinking. We're friends and he was worried about his family. I was just trying to help him feel better."

Truen thought about the information for a moment. "I guess I'm ready to thaw out now."

"Alright then," she said and melted the ice for him. Scithe peeked out from behind the barricade and Truen blasted it with one more fireball. "Okay, Scithe," said Yondel, "*now* it's safe to come out."

"Are you sure?" he called out from behind the wall. Yondel gave Truen a questioning look and Truen nodded grudgingly. "I'm sure, Scithe. Come on out," she said.

The stone barricade crumbled into a pile of gravel and Scithe and Truen sized each other up. Scithe didn't like Truen any more than Truen liked him, but Scithe knew he had not been the good guy in the story. He held out his hand. "Truen, I'm sorry for all the trouble I've caused you and your friends. Will you forgive me?"

"Trouble? That's putting it lightly," Truen muttered. He looked at Yondel who had folded her arms across her chest expectantly. She nodded in the direction of Scithe's outstretched hand.

Truen stared at the hand for a good long minute before taking it. The two shook hands. "And?" Yondel prompted.

"I forgive you," Truen muttered.

"Good!" beamed Yondel hugging both boys in unison. "You've both done really good work today. Let's all be friends." She released them but Truen caught her arm before she could move away.

"Is that how you describe us? Friends?" he asked with a penetrating gaze. She tried to pull her hand away but he wouldn't let her. He gently took her other hand and pulled her close. He looked into her eyes intently, but said nothing for a moment.

Yondel flushed and looked away unable to meet his gaze. "No," she said quietly. Truen tenderly lifted her chin until her eyes met his. "You know we're more than that, Truen," she said.

"Do I? How could I know that?" he asked. She blushed shamefully but couldn't look away. Truen leaned down until his lips were inches from hers.

Scithe cleared his throat loudly. "Still here, guys. Still here." Suddenly self-conscious, Yondel jumped back out of Truen's arms.

"I really hate that guy," Truen muttered.

CHAPTER 11

Granny on a Mission

Granny had not forgotten the night she and Jonuke had first discussed "the plan." Jonuke had come to visit her one night and they had gotten to talking. "You seem to know more about me than I do," Jonuke had said.

"I probably do," she agreed.

"But how?" he asked.

"I'm old Jonuke, so I've been around for a long time. You forget there was a Galvadon before that no good, rotten Karakan parked his high-and-mighty keister here. Before it was against the law, I traveled much and met a lot of people, people that have been long forgotten by most.

"And because of that I know what Galvadon can be, what it's supposed to be and that you're the one that's gonna make it happen. But you can't do it alone. You see, you're not the only one with a mission. In my travels I met some interesting people and one had a gift of seeing things before they happened, a discerner is what he called himself.

"He said that one day I would meet the Vanguard and that I would know him the first time I laid eyes on him. And let me say, he was right about that. I knew you from the moment I saw that odd test of yours!

"He also told me that you would one day rule Galvadon but first the people would need to be united. He said you would accomplish this only with help. I was to help the Vanguard. That was my mission. So, I've always tried to be there for you when you needed my help."

"I've noticed that. Thanks, Granny," said Jonuke sincerely. "I wouldn't be here without you."

She patted his hand. "We need each other and one sign of a good ruler is that he accepts help from those best suited to a task."

"Are you volunteering?" Jonuke asked.

"You betcha!" Granny answered enthusiastically.

"How are we going to do it?" Jonuke asked growing thoughtful. "How are we going to unite Galvadon? The people here just don't get along, especially with the Drek."

"Trust, Jonuke," Granny replied. "They need to learn to trust each other. When you know someone will fight alongside you, you develop a bond with that person that is difficult to break. If the day should come that you need help softening up these hard-headed Elementals, just say the word. We'll call it operation 'tough love.'"

Jonuke chuckled. "I won't ask what that means, but instead thank you in advance for being a true friend that will fight alongside me."

"I'll do what I can to see the land that I love restored to what it can be," Granny replied. She hadn't seen Jonuke since that day and now he was on the run.

Granny had seen terrible things happen to her city and now Galvadon was at an all-time low. The Karakan had taken over completely. The Supreme Council was wanted for treason. The Elite patrolled the city heavily daring the people to disobey their orders. She had become a fugitive who had to keep to the underground tunnels or face arrest.

Granny had made contacts in Galvadon with people she could trust and they organized a meeting for her with several Hydrans who would be most open to change. Her first obstacle was to convince them that they still had a chance, to restore their faith and instill a vision of the Galvadon she yearned for. Most believed all hope was lost.

"The Vanguard is in Galvadon," Granny announced at her first meeting. "If you want your home back, he needs us to stand together. He can't do it alone."

"But the Karakan is too strong," a Hydran argued. "He has the Master's Blade and can't be defeated. We've tried."

"The Vanguard is the rightful ruler of Galvadon. If he defeats the Karakan will you try to work together?" Granny asked.

"Even if we do, how do we know the other Elementals will? We can't do it alone." Granny didn't have answer for them. She didn't know if the others would commit. The meeting ended on flat note.

"Reasoning didn't work," Granny sighed.

"You tried," Oregg replied.

"I guess we'll just have to *show* them how to get along."

*****

The next morning was the same as any other but for the uncanny number of "accidents" that were occurring one right after another. And since shifting was strictly forbidden, no one suspected it was all part of Granny's 'tough love' plan. The Council acted as Granny's little helpers and moved about the city in disguise to carry out the plan.

First, Fantisma sent a gust of wind that blew a Pyrosian family's laundry into the dirt. "Tough love," Fantisma reminded herself as she hurried from the scene. Granny and Phrip just happened to be walking by and offered to help rewash and hang the laundry. The family allowed them to help, but looked at them like they were crazy. They had never seen such behavior. Hydrans helping Pyrosians? Word spread quickly about the strange do-gooders.

Next, Rottmoth shifted a crack up the side of an Aerisian tenement. "Tough love," he said with a smile and disappeared down an alley. Oregg happened upon the distraught tenants and began patching the building without a word. Two giants saw what was happening and joined in with the repairs. The building was patched in no time at all. Rumors spread about the bizarre behavior that was taking place all over Galvadon.

Finally, Phrip shifted a freak rainstorm that flooded a Terran garden. "Tough love," he sighed and walked quickly away. Falnor located Hej and told him as the best gardener in all of Galvadon, they needed his expertise. It wasn't long before Hej was up to his elbows in mulch, replanting the garden.

When a crowd gathered, Granny put them all to work. Some tried to resist pitching in but Granny wouldn't let them. At first there was a lot of awkward silence, but as the work progressed. The Elementals attitudes had warmed significantly.

But then there was an untimely accident. A Terran was working too closely to a Hydran and accidentally elbowed him in the head. "Hey, watch it!" the Hydran shouted.

"You watch it! It's my garden!" the Terran shouted back.

"You're right it is your garden, so you fix it!" yelled the Hydran as he stormed off. Soon petty arguments broke out among everyone and the peace that had been there a moment ago was gone. Soon everyone had left the garden, even the Terrans.

Granny smiled sadly. "Well, it's a start," she said as she rolled up her sleeves and started back in on the garden.

CHAPTER 12

Home Away From Home

J onuke and Sheezu crouched side by side, surveying the area for possible danger. "I don't see anything, Sheez, do you?" The screecher sniffed and shook his head. Sheezu had found Jonuke soon after he had left Galvadon and hadn't left his side since.

Jonuke took a handful of gems from his pouch. They were glowing brightly. "Look!" He held them out for Sheezu to see. "It looks like we're really close to the next gem." He looked around at his treeless surroundings. Great boulders dotted the landscape and large berms of dirt snaked across one another. "I wonder what made those," he wondered aloud.

"I just don't like the feel of this place," he reasoned with Sheezu. "None of the other jewels came easily. If there's one thing I've learned on this quest is to expect the unexpected." Jonuke sighed and considered his options. He didn't have much of a choice here. The other gems had led him to this location and that meant he was very close to the next gem. There was no avoiding it, this was the place.

Memories of invisible predators, collapsing ruins, and booby traps filled his mind. It had been a grueling journey that had tested him to his limits and he'd managed to find all the gems but two. Just then the ground started to shake. "An earthquake?" he said to Sheezu.

Jonuke saw something large plowing through the dirt and heading directly for him. "Well, at least the mystery has been solved about how those berms were made," he said as he leapt onto Sheezu's back and they sprang into the air. Moments later a vianth, a giant worm-like creature, erupted from the ground with its jaws agape. Sheezu dodged the creature as it swung back and forth, attempting to knock them from the air.

Jonuke spied a harness wrapped around its midsection with a small gem sewn into it. He groaned. "On a harness strapped onto a giant worm? Are you kidding me? You know, Sheezu, I'd really like to meet the people that hid these gems and give them a piece of my mind."

Jonuke sighed. "Just two more, Jonuke," he said, giving himself a pep talk. "Two more gems and then you're done." He patted Sheezu. "Let's do this, buddy." Sheezu and Jonuke were as one in thought and action. As the screecher dove for the vianth, Jonuke leapt from his back onto the worm. In one swift move, Jonuke sliced off the harness and threw it over his shoulder. He jumped to the ground and rolled for cover.

Sheezu swiped and pawed at the gargantuan beast to keep it occupied so his partner could escape, but the vianth was only interested in Jonuke. It reared up and threw itself at Jonuke. Eyes flashing silver, Jonuke shifted a shield around himself just as the vianth slammed down on top of him.

It pounded him repeatedly trying to crush him. The hammering drove Jonuke into the ground. "That's how you want to play, huh?" he shouted.

He looked up at the sky and spotted a grey cloud. "That'll do just fine." One benefit from the quest for the gems was that Jonuke was able to practice Energy shifting. Over time he had honed his skill until shifting had become second nature to him.

Shifting the energy particles within the cloud, he sent a bolt of lightning at the beast. The vianth shrieked at the strike but was unmarred. Jonuke used the distraction to run for cover. Enraged, the vianth barreled after him.

"Lightning proof? Okay maybe I underestimated you," Jonuke huffed as he ran for his life. Sheezu flew alongside him and Jonuke climbed aboard. The vianth shot after them, mouth agape. The creature moved faster than Sheezu and its cavernous mouth surrounded them. Jonuke cupped his hands in the shape of a ball and a sphere of energy appeared in them. He pulled his hands apart increasing it to a good size and hurled it down the vianth's throat. The force pushed the creature back down into its tunnel and sent it scurrying away.

"One gem down, one to go," Jonuke smiled patting Sheezu heartily on the back.

*****

Sheezu took them back to the Rhonnadon treasure room where they had found the Master's Blade. This had become a home base for them during their quest for the crown's jewels. Jonuke removed the sparkling pink gem from the harness and studied it closely. "A hundred to one this belongs to the fairies. It's just like them to be difficult.

"Open," Jonuke commanded and treasure room's door opened. He snapped and orbs of light appeared around the room. This was his home away from home, complete with a comfortable king-sized bed, a pitcher of ice-cold water that never ran dry, and platters that filled with any food he requested.

Sheezu plopped down on a down-filled, screecher-sized pillow. "Whatcha in the mood for tonight, boy?" Jonuke asked, holding up an empty platter. Sheezu cocked his head as if he didn't understand the question.

"Let me guess, a steak?" Sheezu licked his lips. "Again? Don't you ever get tired of raw meat?"

Jonuke held the platter firmly with both hands. "One large order of raw meat, please." The plate instantly filled the request and Jonuke delivered the meal to the happy screecher.

"Here you go, but I still think a few veggies now and then would do you good." Sheezu ignored him and focused on his dinner.

Jonuke held up his plate. "I'll have ..." he gave Sheezu a sidelong glance, "a steak, but grilled, not raw." Sheezu stopped eating and glared at Jonuke who held up his hands defensively and said, "*and* a salad." The lettuce appeared on the plate next to the steak. "See? Veggies." He tossed some greens into his mouth. Sheezu just grunted and returned to his meal.

Jonuke took his dinner with him as he walked around the empty treasure room. He pointed at the wall and flicked his wrist sending a cloud of sparks around the room and the once hidden treasure became visible. "There's one more gem out there...." he said thoughtfully. "Let's see... what treasure do I need to take with me this time?" Jonuke nudged a magic carpet with his toe.

"Remember this, Sheez? That was helpful when you injured your wing a few weeks ago. You were scared silly flying around on that thing."

Sheezu sniffed and began his post meal grooming ritual. "What about these automatic inflating arm floaties? It's a good thing we had two pair. That saved us from the whirlpool," Jonuke chuckled at the memory. "You have to admit you looked pretty funny though, floating around helplessly with a pair of arm floaties stuck to your arms." Sheezu growled. "Alright, alright. I'll stop.

"The real question is what we are going to need to help us on our quest for the final gem?" His eyes searched the countless treasures and then came to rest on a carved wooden dragon. "What's this?" asked Jonuke as he studied it closely.

"I think it's a whistle," he brought it to his lips and blew. The whistle made a low baleful sound that made Sheezu cock his head with interest. "That's not the sound I expected from this little thing. I wonder what it's for."

Suddenly, Sheezu scrambled to his feet and growled at the entrance to the treasure room. "What's wrong?" Jonuke asked.

There was a massive beating of wings and the great dragon Shayzah peered into the room. "You called, Vanguard?" he rasped.

CHAPTER 13

A Gift

Sheezu crouched on the ready for an attack. "It's alright, boy," Jonuke reassured. "Shayzah's a friend. Stay put until I get back." Jonuke ducked out of the cave to speak with the dragon.

"The time nears for the return of the Rhonnadon," began Shayzah. "It appears you again require my help. Come with me."

Jonuke climbed onto the dragon's back and they took to the air. "You see, the Rhonnadon have largely been forgotten. Not only as the great rulers of Galvadon, but their ways are no longer practiced among your people. Until the Elementals are willing to trust as you have learned to do, they will not be ready for the return of the Rhonnadon."

"Where are they ... the Rhonnadon?" Jonuke asked.

"They are not as far as you might think, but you will not find them until you truly understand your mission."

"But I know what I need to do. I am searching for the crown so I can defeat the Karakan, unify Galvadon, and bring the nine kingdoms together."

"The Crown of Rulers will not unify Galvadon. You must do that, but you cannot do it alone. You already know this and have sought the help of the Elemental, Edween. I see hearts beginning to soften. That is good. But it is still not enough. *You* must gain the trust of your people."

"How can I do that?" Jonuke asked. "I'm a fugitive and a Drek. You have to agree that the odds are against me."

"Look!" The dragon had taken them back to Galvadon. Jonuke saw the abandoned cities, the tenements, the great wall around the city, and the lost hope in people's faces. He saw giants, gnomes, dwarves, all people of all Lands together in Galvadon.

"It appears your work has been done for you," Shayzah scoffed. "The Karakan has brought the nine kingdoms together."

A Gift

Jonuke was a little confused at first. Yes, this was what he had wanted. He had envisioned everyone together, but this wasn't what it was supposed to look like. "No. That's not right. The people are together, but—" Jonuke started.

"But it is what you said you wanted," the dragon replied.

"Not like this. They aren't happy. No one is smiling," Jonuke observed.

"Why do you think that is so?" asked Shayzah.

"They clearly don't want to be here. The Karakan has walled them in. He is forcing them to stay. They are slaves," explained Jonuke.

"Yes. But they are working together for the greater good. Each is using his strengths to enhance the whole. Shouldn't this make them happy?" Shayzah was pushing Jonuke to make an important distinction.

Jonuke thought about what the dragon was saying. At face value, it sounded like a good idea, everyone living together, working together. They should be happy, but they weren't. They were clearly miserable. Their homes were drab and colorless, the gnomes made the clothing for everyone, but it was nothing like what they made for him as a gift. Their hearts just weren't in their work. Why? The answer came to his mind readily. "They aren't free. They're prisoners," he said aloud.

"Remember what you see here today and let it remind you of the importance of a man's right to choose. Agency is everything. Choosing the good brings happiness while choosing evil brings misery. If agency is taken away, you are left with this." Shayzah indicated the current state of Galvadon. "It always has been and always will be," said the dragon wisely.

Shayzah set a course back to the treasure room. This time they flew low beneath the clouds and Jonuke saw the castle he had visited not long ago. *That was odd*, he thought. Shayzah had chosen an indirect route back to the treasure room. He wondered if the dragon had intended for him to see this castle.

"I have shown you what I must," said Shayzah when they had returned. "Our paths will not cross again until the kingdom is at peace and the Rhonnadon have returned."

"Thank you for what you have shown me," said Jonuke.

Shayzah turned to leave but then stopped. "I feel there is something else I must give you. Do you remember the dragon scale of the Great Dragon, Zanu?"

Jonuke remembered. It had been very difficult for him to look into the scale and learn things about himself that he needed to change. Hard things.

"Dragon scales are as different as the dragons from which they come. They have special properties that even

A Gift

the dragons do not fully understand. I wish to make you a gift of one of mine." Shayzah removed one of his metallic aqua scales and pierced the end with his claw. "Wear it about your neck and its purpose will be made known to you when the time is right. Farewell, young Vanguard." With that, Shayzah flew away.

Jonuke obediently threaded the scale onto the chain with his mother's locket that he always wore around his neck and wondered at the purpose of the scale.

When Jonuke walked into the treasure room, he found Sheezu in a meat bliss coma. Jonuke didn't like to startle the animal for obvious reasons but nap time was over. "Wake up, Sheez," he called softly. Sheezu didn't budge. Jonuke clapped his hands loudly but his friend was out cold. Judging from the twitches and snorts, he was dreaming of an exciting chase.

Jonuke took cover behind the bed and gave Sheezu a small zap in the hind quarters that nearly sent him through the ceiling. "You're losing your edge, big guy," Jonuke chuckled as the screecher yawned and stretched. "You really need to lay off the second helpings. Come on, I think we're supposed to revisit that old castle I told you about.

CHAPTER 14

A Helpful Hint

Jonuke peered into the castle remembering the last time he was here. He barely escaped with his life after being chased down by an army of stone gargantuans. He looked on either side of the entry way and the guards weren't there this time. *Hmm*, he wondered. Where were they?

He looked around the room and noticed the hole in the wall was still there from his narrow escape. He hoped he wouldn't need to use that exit again. He knew he had to be insane to return here on a mere hunch, but that's how he rolled these days.

Jonuke cautiously explored the castle. He climbed the stairs to the library but nothing in particular caught his interest this time. He poked his head into the room with a painting of a man on the wall. He recognized him this time. It was the younger version of the Rhonnadon who had visited him in the treasure room for the very first time. *What was his portrait doing here?* And then it dawned on him. This castle belonged to the Rhonnadon and was probably where they had resided when they ruled Galvadon.

He didn't know why he hadn't seen it before. It all made sense. That's why the granite guardians recognized that he was an Energy shifter! He turned to leave the room, but there blocking the doorway was one of the gargantuans.

"Speak the password," it demanded.

Jonuke was prepared for this. The same thing had happened the last time he was here, so he had had time to think about it and was feeling pretty sure of himself. Shayzah had made it clear that the people needed to be unified, not just together. "Unity," Jonuke declared.

"That is incorrect," the sentry replied.

"Agency, the right to choose," Jonuke tried as a giant hand came at him.

"Incorrect," the sentry said again.

Dodging its grasp, he tried other passwords that had worked in the past, "Jonuke of Londor."

"That is incorrect." The hand swiped at him again.

"The Vanguard," Jonuke tried ducking the hand.

"Incorrect."

As a last ditch effort, he tried to reason with the guard in the ancient tongue. *"Veh may Vanguard ton forro raniah mahn Rhonnadon."* *I'm the Vanguard here to bring back the Rhonnadon.*

At last the stone hand succeeded in grabbing Jonuke and brought him out of the room. "That is incorrect. You were unwise to return here."

Jonuke shifted Energy into the hand hoping to loosen the grip but it had no effect. The guard carried him down the stairs into the great entryway. This time there were dozens of stone sentries lining the walls. "That the secret of the Rhonnadon may be kept, you will never leave this place." Even the hole in the wall was blocked. The guard dropped Jonuke in the center of the room

"The secret of the Rhonnadon?" Jonuke muttered. "What is that supposed to mean?" He searched the main floor for a way out but all the exits were blocked.

"Well, if I'm stuck here, I might as well make the most of my time. He walked up the stairs and considered reading a book from the library. "I'll have time enough for that later," he decided. The field guide to the Darke Forest would be an interesting read, he thought to himself.

He thought he would explore the different rooms in the castle to see if there were any clues as to what password the granite guardians wanted to hear. Most of the rooms were bedrooms, but one in particular caught his interest. It was much larger than the others and had the biggest bed he'd ever seen.

He was sure that the room had been lavishly decorated in its day. Though dusty and moth-eaten, the fabrics were rich and the carpets were thick. Crown molding framed the bejeweled ceiling. Fancy wall paper lined the walls. There was a painting of a man on an easel in the corner of the room. The painting depicted a man with shoulder length white hair who wore plain brown clothing. The picture didn't seem to match the rest of the room. Jonuke would have expected to see the picture of a king here.

As Jonuke approached the painting, the ring on his finger began to glow brightly. The ring had belonged to Galvadon's last great leader, Mahlneer, and had given Jonuke access to the hidden kingdoms of the fairies and the Palean. The fact that it was glowing right now had to indicate that he was near a doorway of some kind.

"Hello, Jonuke," the man in the painting said amiably. Jonuke nearly jumped out of his skin at hearing the painting call him by name.

"How do you know me?" Jonuke asked.

"You are the Vanguard, are you not?" the man replied.

"Yes," Jonuke answered. "Who are you?"

"Gannon, the leader of the Rhonnadon, but is that the information you desire most of me?" he asked.

"I don't suppose you know the password those stone thugs at the bottom of the stairs are looking for?" asked Jonuke.

"I do," Gannon answered simply.

"Can you tell me?" Jonuke asked.

"No. It is something you must know within your heart. The good news is that the password is already written on your heart, you just haven't discovered it yet."

"Great, another mind game." Jonuke deliberated over what the password might be.

"Would you like a hint?" Gannon offered.

"I thought you couldn't help me," replied Jonuke.

"No, I didn't say that. I said I couldn't *tell* you. Helping you is totally legal," Gannon smiled. "My clue to you is this:

You first learned from a dragon,
Then from Elementals of fire and ice,
Finally, a wise woman reminded you once more.

Jonuke didn't complain about the riddle, he just sighed. He had come to accept the fact that the Rhonnadon didn't have the ability to speak like normal human beings.

"The dragon is Shayzah, fire and ice are Truen and Yondel, and the wise woman is Granny," Jonuke concluded.

"Good!" the man in the painting said proudly. "Your skills at riddles have greatly improved. Now what do they all have in common? They all taught you something that was difficult for you to learn," he prompted.

Jonuke thought back to what the dragon had taught him about relying on his friends. He thought about how Truen and Yondel had risked their lives for him repeatedly. And then he remembered what Granny had said was the key to uniting Galvadon. "Trust," Jonuke said aloud.

"That is correct!" Jonuke heard the voices of the stone sentinels reply in unison from the ground floor.

"Now hurry downstairs and I'll see you shortly," Gannon said and then he became still once more.

Jonuke ran down to the main floor and saw the sentinels marching to the center of the room. Jonuke watched as the guards began to break apart. The pieces flew up into the air and swirled around the room. Then the parts began to snap back together with an ear-ringing *crack, crack, crack* until they had formed an enormous ring that rested vertically on the floor. When Jonuke looked through the center of the ring, he saw a land he'd never seen before. *The Forgotten Kingdom of the Rhonnadon.* He stepped into the ring and disappeared.

CHAPTER 15

Meet Nya

Jonuke spiraled through space like he was being flushed down a drain and then suddenly he was standing in the entry way of the castle, but it was different. It was immaculate and looked brand new. The threadbare carpets were thick and bright. Instead of being covered in cobwebs, the pillars sparkled. Intricately woven tapestries hung from the walls and were free of dust. Servants bustled around the castle cleaning, sweeping, and washing.

"Welcome, Vanguard!" Gannon came down the stairway and met Jonuke. "We have been expecting you."

"Father?" A beautiful girl about Jonuke's age walked into the entryway. Thick dark curls framed her fair complexion and she wore a pale blue gown that was tailored snugly around the bodice and flared out loosely at the hip fitting her slim figure nicely. "You called for me?" She asked with a ready smile.

"I wanted you to meet our visitor, Jonuke," he said. "Jonuke this is my daughter Nya."

"A visitor?" Nya's bright green eyes lit up with genuine interest at meeting the newcomer. "How wonderful!"

"Pleased to meet you, Nya," Jonuke replied.

"Nya, I was hoping that you would show Jonuke around our city," Gannon suggested. "He is from Galvadon and I believe he would be very interested in seeing how things work around here."

"I would love to, Father," she said graciously and led Jonuke out of the castle and into the surrounding city.

"Galvadon ..." she began thoughtfully. "I have heard so much about your land. Tell me everything." Jonuke explained what Galvadon had been with all the amazing talents of the Elementals and what it had become after the Karakan had taken over.

"Oh, I'm sorry to hear that. The Elders say someday we will return to Galvadon, that a Vanguard is prophesied to bring peace. Do you think that will be soon?" she asked.

This is awkward, Jonuke thought. She clearly didn't know *he* was the Vanguard. He considered saying, *Yeah, that's me. I'm the guy.* But it didn't sound right in his head, so he just nodded and said, "Yes, very soon."

She gave him a detailed tour of the city. "Everyone here is gifted, just like Galvadon. But our gifts are much more varied. "My gift is to communicate with animals. Like with Ponpon here." She beckoned a long necked creature with floppy ears and a poofy tuft of hair atop its head.

"He would like to know if you want to pat his head," she said to Jonuke. "He particularly likes that, you know."

Jonuke patted the animal's head amiably. "It's very nice to meet you, Ponpon." The creature nuzzled his hand and trotted away.

"He said he likes you. That's quite a compliment coming from him," she explained.

"I'm glad I met with Ponpon's approval," Jonuke chuckled.

"He also said you are more than what you appear. I wonder what he meant by that?" she asked looking him over quizzically.

Awkward was back. *Why couldn't he just say he was the Vanguard?* He argued with himself. *Because he didn't want to sound like he was trying to impress her.* He replied to himself. *Why did he care what she thought?* He rebutted. He didn't know, but he cared very much. "Hopefully something good," he replied lamely.

The tour continued. "We work together, trading for what we need." They walked by farms with the largest yields he'd ever seen. Not only in quantity, but the size of the produce was abnormally large, like what one might see in the giant's village.

"What does one trade for the services of an animal whisperer?" Jonuke asked curiously.

Nya blushed. "I kinda like that...animal whisperer," she said repeating the term Jonuke had invented. "I live in the castle and am being tutored in leadership skills most of the time, but I'm happy to volunteer my services for any animal problems that may arise."

"Animal problems?" Jonuke asked.

"Last week angry pildrees threatened the city and I talked to them and calmed them down before they did any damage," she explained.

Jonuke had a hard time imagining this slight young woman facing anything very dangerous, especially as one who was used to palace life.

Nya read this thoughts like a book. "You don't believe me, do you?" She whistled and a large hairy beast lumbered over to them on four legs. Jonuke was very uncomfortable when it roared and snarled baring its sharp fangs. "Is that threatening enough for you?" she smirked.

"Definitely. I shouldn't have doubted a Rhonnadonian princess," Jonuke smiled. Satisfied she thanked the pildree for the demonstration and sent it back to wherever it came from.

Nya asked Jonuke about his life in the forest and she surprised him by having quite a knowledge of the Darke Forest. When he asked her about how she knew so much, she told him she had studied the journals of various explorers as a hobby and eventually compiled them.

"Have you ever seen a grumlot?" Nya asked.

"Unfortunately, I've had several unpleasant run-ins," Jonuke replied.

"Well, did you know that if you approach the grumlot from behind while singing, the animal becomes quite docile and may be scratched behind the ears?" she asked.

Jonuke remembered reading that exact phrase in a book he had found in the Rhonnadonian library the first time he had visited. He looked at Nya with disbelief. "*You* wrote the field guide to the Darke Forest?"

It was Nya's turn to look surprised. "How did you know that?"

Jonuke laughed and shook his head. He explained how he'd discovered the book and just happened to turn to that very page. "What a coincidence, huh?"

"There are no coincidences," Nya replied matter-of-factly but wasn't significant about it. She continued the tour of her city telling him about all the plants and animals that were here and how they were similar to those in Galvadon. He enjoyed hearing all she had to tell him and he found that he liked Nya very much, especially how she knew what he was thinking before he did. She was easy to talk to and they found they had similar interests.

The feeling of the Forgotten Kingdom was one of peace and contentment. The people living here, the Rhonnadon, smiled and seemed to get along well. It was something Jonuke had never seen in Galvadon.

The city itself was beautifully designed. It had been created from a master plan and gave the impression of unity and cooperation. Fountains burst from every corner of the city reflecting a rainbow of color in their mist. The most varied creative architecture was used on a variety of structures. Some spiraled up to the sky in a point like a sea shell while others were fluffy and round like a giant cotton ball.

Jonuke saw flyers, builders, chefs that could change a pile of dirt into a feast, gardeners, a healer, those with the ability to disappear, and others to move as quickly as the dwarves. He saw one who was able to mold solid objects like they were made of clay into various forms and another organize a messy space with a snap of the fingers. But what stood out most to Jonuke was their willingness to drop whatever they were doing to help one another. Their society was the opposite of what Galvadon had become and Jonuke said as much to Nya.

"We truly live in abundance. I hope we can one day bring this to Galvadon," she said. They had come back to the castle and were standing on the front steps. "So, what's your gift?" Nya asked.

"Energy shifter," Jonuke replied.

"Really?" she asked looking impressed. "I didn't know they had those in Galvadon. They are really rare even here. The Elders say that when an Energy Shifter is born in Galvadon ..." She was silent for a minute and Jonuke watched the wheels turning in her mind. "Wait a minute ..." she looked at Jonuke accusingly. "You're the Vanguard, aren't you?" Jonuke nodded sheepishly.

"Why didn't you tell me when I asked you about it earlier?" she asked reproachfully.

"Don't be too hard on him, Nya," said Gannon as he walked down the steps to meet them. "This is all still fairly new to Jonuke and you're a pretty girl. He didn't want to appear a braggart." Then to Jonuke he said, "Come. Let us discuss the next part of your mission." The three of them walked up the steps and back into the entry.

"A mission?" Nya repeated letting the matter of Jonuke's surprising identity drop. "That's right! You are destined to unite Galvadon and bring the Rhonnadon home. After reading about it in our history books for all of these years, I can't believe the time has finally arrived. How exciting! I wish such an adventure was in my future," she said wistfully.

Gannon beamed at his daughter's enthusiasm. "I'm sure there is much adventure in your future, honey. I am glad to see you and Jonuke are getting on so well. I wanted you two to get to know one another before I told you."

The smile on Nya's face faded to a look of suspicion. She knew her father and it wasn't unlike him to spring schemes on her, that she may or may not like. "Told me what?" she asked guardedly.

"When you were born," he began, "it was prophesied that you would one day wed the one that sought us out and brought us home, the Vanguard." He smiled proudly looking at the both of them.

Both Jonuke and Nya looked stunned. They glanced at each other awkwardly and took a step apart. Jonuke cleared his throat, "Uh, don't you think we're a little young to be talking about marriage?"

Nya nodded vigorously her agreement, "Yeah, that," she said pointing at Jonuke.

Gannon just laughed. "Not today, you two. Years in the future, as many as you like. You have time."

"Still, Father," Nya piped up, "I think some things are better left unsaid. Now I can't even look at the guy without feeling awkward."

Jonuke was glad she said what he was thinking. Nya turned to Jonuke and said, "So, Jonuke, prophecy or no, I hereby release you from our betrothal. You are free to one day marry whomever you choose and I plan to do the same. Deal?" Nya held her hand out to shake on the contract.

"Deal," Jonuke sighed in relief and took her hand. As soon as their hands met a spark shot out from between their clasped hands, and the two quickly released their grasp.

"Sparks are flying. Resistance is futile," Gannon said simply.

"Ignore my dad, Jonuke. I think he may be losing his mind," Nya teased. "Before he says anything else that I'm sure to regret, I'll say my goodbyes and excuse myself to take care of any urgent animal whispering business that may come up. It was a pleasure, Sir Vanguard," she said with a twinkle in her eye and bowed with exaggerated respect before leaving the room.

"Oh, she'll come around," Gannon promised. "I've yet to see an unfulfilled prophecy." He smiled at Jonuke who was feeling very uncomfortable with this topic. "Now to business. How is the quest for the crown coming? Let's see the gems you've found."

Jonuke poured the gems into his hand and held them out for Gannon to look at. "I was hoping you had the final gem," Jonuke said.

"Oh, no. Ours was buried with King Mahlneer and I see you already have that one," he said pointing to the clear rectangular gem. "No, the one you are missing belongs to a people near extinction. I believe only two of their kind remain."

"How will I find them?" Jonuke asked.

"Don't worry about that one. That gem is not ready to be found at this time and will present itself to you when the time is right. For now you must find the crown."

"That is what concerns me," Jonuke replied. "I was hoping that once I found all of the gems, they would lead me to the crown."

"Finding the crown isn't going to be a problem. It's located on that mountain peak," Gannon said pointing to the mountain not far from where they were standing. "It's proving that you are ready to wear the crown that will be your greatest challenge. Only one who has all the qualities of a strong ruler can wear the Crown of Rulers. Do you feel that you are ready?" Jonuke wasn't sure, but he didn't have much of a choice. Galvadon needed him.

"I understand your predicament, Jonuke," Gannon said. "Ready or not you must try to obtain the crown, but be careful, if you do not succeed, you will not get a second chance."

CHAPTER 16

Consequences

Hiking the mountain was the easy part. Jonuke entered the cave at its peak. The cave was dark save a stream of light that shone from an opening in the ceiling. The light illuminated the crown that sat on a pedestal at the far end of the cave. The crown was his for the taking? Jonuke was seasoned enough at questing to know it couldn't be that easy and was instantly on his guard. Jonuke took a slow step toward the crown.

"He who desires the crown must prove he is worthy through a series of tests," echoed a voice through the cave but Jonuke didn't see anyone.

"Of course I do," Jonuke muttered and shook his head at the predictability of the situation. But what he wasn't expecting was the small troll dressed in boxing shorts that stepped out from behind the pedestal. He was holding a large cone to his mouth that he was using as a megaphone to amplify his voice.

"Bravery, skill, and wisdom are what is required to obtain the Crown of Rulers," the little troll's voice echoed through the cave.

Jonuke couldn't help but snicker at the sight of the little troll with the big voice. "You can't be serious," he said. Torches lit around the room revealing a boxing ring at its center.

The troll dropped the megaphone and climbed into the ring. "Com'ear, pretty boy, and I'll wipe that smile off your face," he growled. "Or aren't you brave enough to face someone half your size?"

Jonuke hesitated before climbing into the ring. Something about this seemed all wrong. The troll threw a few practice punches, danced around Jonuke beckoning him to fight.

Jonuke held up his fists and looked down at the troll. "I can't. It's not a fair fight. I don't want to hurt you."

"Well, if you won't throw the first punch, I will. Let it be noted you've lost a point for wisdom." Jonuke was unprepared for what happened next.

The troll stomped his foot and expanded before Jonuke's eyes until he towered over him. "Is this better?" the troll boomed, lifting his massive foot to squash his opponent. Jonuke dove out of the way just as the foot came crashing down.

The troll lumbered toward Jonuke and tried to kick him but Jonuke dodged and shifted a large crackling ball of energy in his hands and hurled it at the troll.

"Oof!" the troll groaned but shook it off quickly and swung a giant fist at Jonuke. Instead of dodging the fist, Jonuke grabbed hold and climbed up the troll's arm. The troll waved his arm wildly, trying to shake Jonuke off, but he held firm. Jonuke climbed up to the troll's shoulders and said, "Let's not do this. I don't want to hurt you, and we both know I'm going to win this fight, anyway."

"Feeling confident are we?" the troll replied. "You better have something up your sleeve that is going to really impress me then."

Jonuke jumped back down into the ring and faced the troll. He backed up slowly until he was up against the elastic ropes that surrounded the ring. "What are you going to do now?" the troll taunted. "You're losing points by the minute.

The troll dove for Jonuke and the Vanguard leapt out of the ring. The troll tumbled up against the ropes. Focusing the Energy on the strength of his arms, Jonuke pulled the elastic rope back and catapulted the giant troll out of the boxing ring. The troll smashed against a wall and landed in a heap on the ground.

Dazed, he rubbed his head and got to his feet. "Wowie, zowie! You've got skills, boy," the troll congratulated while looking quite impressed. "I've never seen that move before. You earn an A+ on your skills test. And you earned a bonus point in the bravery category for style and another for the trash talk you did back there."

The troll shrunk back down to his previous size. "Much better," he said to himself and then to Jonuke, "But your wisdom is still in question. I'll have to devise an entirely new test for that." His hand went to his chin, and he pulled at his scraggly beard while he considered several different possibilities.

"I've got it!" he said thrusting a finger into the air. He snapped his fingers and the boxing ring disappeared. He clapped his hands together and a pit of venomous snakes appeared in its place. He pulled his ear and the pedestal began to slowly lower into the ground.

"You see, as the guardian of the crown, I need to know that you are going to make wise decisions, that you have your priorities straight. Are you going to save the crown, which is symbolic of your kingdom or your girlfriend?"

"Girlfriend?" said Jonuke looking confused.

"Oh!" the troll said slapping his forehead. "I almost forgot. The troll wore a necklace with a glass orb on the end. He pulled off the necklace and smashed the glass ball on the ground filling the room with smoke.

Both Jonuke and the troll coughed and sputtered. "Sorry about that," the troll wheezed. "I like to use the necklace for dramatic effect, but I'm starting to think it just isn't worth it."

When the smoke cleared, Jonuke saw Nya securely bound and suspended by a single rope from the ceiling over the pit of snakes. "Jonuke?" Nya said anxiously as she grasped the gravity of the perilous situation she was in.

The troll picked up the megaphone and said ominously, "Who will you save, the kingdom or your girlfriend?" The troll let the megaphone drop to his side and added, "And no, you can't have them both. It's a test. You have to choose."

"Wait a minute? Girlfriend?" Nya asked as the rope began to unwind, lowering her into the pit of snakes. "Did you tell the troll what my father said? I thought we had an agreement?"

Jonuke didn't have time to respond. Nya was almost in reach of the snakes and the crown was disappearing before his eyes. "*Uma lo rey danah mahk!*" An energy shield appeared as a barrier between Nya and the snakes just as a viper hissed and darted for her ankle. Sparks shot out from the shield electrocuting the attacker. Jonuke grabbed the hunting knife at his shoulder and threw it at the rope. The knife sliced through the rope as Jonuke dove over the pit, grabbing Nya, and tumbling with her to the ground on the other side of the pit.

The crown was just sinking into the ground. Jonuke reached out in the direction of the crown and shifted the Energy around it so it flew into his hand.

"Nya, are you …?" Jonuke started, but she was gone.

"Man, I told you, you gotta follow the rules! You can't have both. Sometimes you have to choose. Not a very wise one are you? Fail, fail, faaaiiil! Now you lose everything and you have only yourself to blame."

The troll snapped his fingers and the crown disappeared from his grasp and reappeared on the platform at the far end of the cave. Jonuke was so distraught at the surprising turn of events, he didn't see the troll point at an especially large red striped snake.

"You'll do just fine," the troll said, wiggling his nose and levitating the snake out of the pit. Jonuke glanced over just in time to see the snake bite him on the ankle. The poison worked quickly, spreading throughout Jonuke's body. He felt his head spinning and then he lost consciousness.

CHAPTER 17

He Knows

Jonuke was aware of darkness all around him and then of a voice calling his name. "Jonuke. Don't worry. You will be made whole again." He realized that he recognized the voice. It was soft and peaceful and familiar. It was a voice he had heard many times before. Counseling him, warning him, teaching him. But although he recognized it, he couldn't quite remember who it belonged to.

Then a light appeared next to him. It was blurred at first but came slowly into focus. A woman stood next to him. It was the woman from his dreams, the one he had seen so many times before. He'd forgotten about the many times she had visited him, but now the memories came back.

She had taught him the tongue of Rhonnadon. She had taught him to heal. She had always been there when he was hurt or sad to comfort him. As she placed her hand over his wounded ankle, he felt the healing warmth replace the pain of the poison. The warmth traveled throughout his body, healing as it went until the effects of the poison had been completely reversed.

Jonuke's eyes flew open and he sat up. Had it all been a dream? He looked around at the empty cave. He saw the crown on the pedestal but the troll and the snakes were gone. He lifted his pant leg and examined his ankle. No, the bite mark was still there but was now just two small round scars. He felt eyes on him and he turned around.

There stood the woman that had healed him. This time he knew who she was. "Mom?" he said.

There were tears running down her cheeks. "How I've missed you, Jonuke!"

"What happened to you? Why did you leave?" he asked, struggling to his feet.

"I shouldn't be here," she replied. "I've stayed too long," she said backing away.

"Don't go!" pleaded Jonuke. "I can help you. Whatever trouble you're in. I can help."

"You have come so far, Jonuke, and I am so proud of you! But there is more to do before we can be a family again," she tried to explain in a way he could understand why she couldn't come with him now.

"I don't understand. Why did you leave dad? Why did you leave me?" Jonuke asked with emotion that he could no longer hold back.

"Is that what you think? All these years ... that I left?" Tears welled up in her eyes. "I would never leave my family, Jonuke."

"Then come with me now." He took a step forward and reached out for her.

Linayah jumped back as if she were afraid of his touch. "No, Jonuke. You cannot touch me. It is for your own safety that I have to go now. It is your destiny to bring peace to Galvadon. Someday I will find my way back home," she said sadly as she turned to go.

"Let me help." His hand shot out to grasp hers but passed right through it. He discovered that his mother wasn't actually in the room with him. Jonuke realized he'd been looking at an ethereal image of his mother.

"Linayah?" came a man's voice. "Where are you, Linayah?"

"Wait. You aren't really here? Where are you?" asked Jonuke trying to make sense of the situation.

"No, Jonuke!" she said in dismay. "Now he knows. I shouldn't have come here. Quick, you must go! We both must leave this place immediately!"

Just then an ethereal image of the Karakan appeared next to his mother. "It's too late for that, Linayah. You know better than that. Now what have you been up to?" He turned and looked at Jonuke. The Karakan slowly circled Jonuke looking him over curiously.

"But why would you take such a chance to visit a Drek on the run?" He looked thoughtfully at Jonuke and then at Linayah. "You're out of practice, dearest. Your fear tells me everything...You have a son? This boy is your *son* ...? I see the resemblance now .... How were you able to keep this from me—? Wait a minute!" he said looking into her mind again. "You married Londor?!" he shouted with a grimace. "How could you?" He looked at her accusingly. "And ... you've been sneaking out behind my back to visit him! How?" the Karakan demanded.

"You forget who I am," Linayah replied. "I have abilities you never understood. You only see fear, power, and control. Anything motivated by love and genuine concern for another will always be foreign to you." She finished straightening to her full height. Jonuke thought she looked magnificent and regal, like a queen. She wasn't afraid of what the Karakan might do to her, but she worried about Jonuke.

"You have been far too much trouble for one day," said the Karakan. "Back to where you belong. Back to your tower." Linayah looked sadly at Jonuke and then disappeared.

"Let her go!" Jonuke shouted. "Where have you sent her?"

"Oh she's quite safe and somewhere you will never find her." He laughed but then stopped abruptly. "Wait another minute. I recognize this place." He looked across the room at the crown. "What are *you* doing *here* with the Crown of Rulers?"

His eyes went to Jonuke's hand and grew wide with recognition. "Mahlneer's ring! You...?" He remembered the vision he had seen of the Vanguard holding the sword and the ring he had seen on his finger. The ring matched the one on Jonuke's hand. "You're... the Vanguard?" he asked incredulously. He was silent for a moment as all the pieces of the puzzle fell into place.

"Londor's and Linayah's son ... the test in the arena that didn't make sense ... breaking my laws and leaving Galvadon .... I should have seen it sooner. It is so clear to me now. Well, well, well," he said circling Jonuke again and looking at him with new eyes. "Jonuke of Londor is the Vanguard, huh? It appears the fun is just beginning."

"I'd like that ring," the Karakan said almost as an afterthought. Jonuke looked down at the ring on his finger. There was no way he was going to give it to the Karakan.

"Oh, I didn't really expect you to give it to me," the Karakan explained. "You see magical objects are attracted to one another. The more powerful the object, the stronger the attraction." He unsheathed the sword at his waist.

"Do you know what this is?" asked the Karakan. But before Jonuke could answer, the Karakan answered for him. "Of course you do. It used to be in your possession not long ago, didn't it?" He held up the sword admiring it. "It is beautiful, isn't it?" The Karakan pointed the sword at the crown and it flew across the room into his hand.

Jonuke knew he had to get that sword. Now that the crown was gone, it was his last chance to save Galvadon from the Karakan. Focusing his energy on the sword, he tried to loose it from the Karakan's grasp, but nothing happened. Then he sent an energy blast at the Karakan, but again, nothing happened.

"An Energy shifter? Impressive! I haven't seen one of those since—" he paused. "I can't remember the last time.

"Normally, the sword would have done you some serious harm for trying to attack me, but it seems to have escaped your attention that I am not actually in this cave with you. Like your mother, I'm just visiting. So, we'll have to play the try-and-take-the-sword-game another day.

"But what I'm really interested in right now is that ring. My men have not been able to enter two of the hidden kingdoms and I believe that ring will prove very helpful in that endeavor." He pointed the sword at Jonuke's hand and the ring slid off his finger and onto the Karakan's hand.

"Until we meet again, Vanguard." The Karakan vanished and Jonuke was left alone in the cave.

CHAPTER 18

Mind Games

"Why didn't you just dispose of him when you had the chance?" asked Silvane as he and the Karakan watched Jonuke in the crystal table from his chambers. At the Karakan's command, the table showed all the goings on in the land—save the Darke Forest—and an occasional instant replay of those events.

"Where's the fun in that?" the Karakan asked.

"Fun? Is this some sort of game for you?" Silvane asked incredulously.

"Of course it is! I'm surprised at you, Silvane. I would have thought you had figured that out by now.

Why else would I paint my enemies into a picture and watch them struggle? Their fears have betrayed them all.

"I painted the ants so large around that giant, Grog, that he thinks he has shrunk to the size of a flea! Funny, right? And that wolf-warrior, Wardek? He thinks his son-in-law, Belzar, has come back to life and moved in with him. Hilarious! That's what I call entertainment!" the Karakan said slapping his knee for emphasis.

"Don't get me wrong, Silvane. I don't like to lose and I can be quite a poor sport if it appears that might happen." The Karakan paced back and forth for a moment.

"Now as for the Vanguard... he's different than the others. I don't want to risk having him get away and somehow fulfilling that stupid prophecy. Him, I will dispose of. He's been such a pain in the neck traipsing all over the Forbidden Lands. Now that I know his identity, I have great influence over his mind. Let's just see if I can't have a little fun and solve my Vanguard problem at the same time," he said thoughtfully. "There's a particularly dangerous part of the forest near that castle, if I remember correctly, that has our clueless hero's name written all over it," he grinned wickedly.

"As for our conquests, there are two more kingdoms we have not seized, hidden kingdoms. Find the fairy kingdom while I finish up with the Vanguard." The Karakan handed Silvane a golden feather. "When you have found the fairies, this will allow me to travel to your location instantly and we will conquer them like we did the others." The Karakan patted the sword at his waist.

Silvane took the feather. "It shall be as you instruct, Great Karakan."

*****

I have your mother, Jonuke, the Karakan's thoughts forced their way into Jonuke's mind.

What did the Karakan want with his mother? Jonuke thought. There was nothing he could do to help her. This feeling of powerlessness brought fear into his heart and opened the flood gate for more of the Karakan's thoughts.

Her life is in my hands, came the Karakan's threat. The fear began to take control of Jonuke, and his surroundings started to change. It was like he was in the testing arena all over again. The Karakan had access to his mind and he had no power to stop it. His mind grew clouded until he was only cognizant of his new surroundings.

Jonuke found himself in a grassy field and his mother was calling to him. She was tied to a tree on the other side of a pool of water. He had to get to her. Jonuke had an uneasy feeling about the water. He peered into the pond and could easily see to the bottom. It looked like average water to him. There weren't any creatures in it, not even fish, so there was no threat there. He shrugged off the warning bells in his head. The water extended as far as the eye could see, so there was no way around it. He was going to have to swim across.

*****

After the thrill of being lowered into a pit of poisonous snakes, Nya had decided that she was way overdo for an adventure and had followed Jonuke through the portal and into the Darke Forest. She had just gotten up the courage to tell him that she was coming with him when she saw him standing on the edge of a pool of quicksand. *What was he doing?* She wondered. She called out to him, but he didn't answer. He seemed to be in some kind of trance. Before she could get to him, he leapt into the quicksand and immediately began to sink. Thinking quickly, she took a rope from her belt, secured it to a tree, and dove in after him.

*****

As soon as Nya touched him, Jonuke came back to his senses and realized he was sinking in quicksand. He grabbed onto her and they worked together to pull themselves out to solid ground. Both coughed and sputtered sand and took a moment to catch their breath.

"Are you okay?" Nya asked with a look of concern. "You were under for a while."

Jonuke nodded. "Thanks for being in the right place at the right time."

"What were you doing? I saw you dive into that quicksand like you thought it was a swimming pool."

"That's basically what I thought it was, a clear blue swimming pool," Jonuke replied. "I was under the impression that I had to get across it to save my mom."

Nya looked around. "Your mom?" But there was no one there but them. She looked perplexed for a minute but then her eyes brightened. "Oh, a mind shifter."

"A what?"

"You're under the influence of a mind shifter. I've seen stuff like this before but only as a prank, never so deadly."

Jonuke explained about the Karakan's ability to get into one's mind and how he'd taken the crown and imprisoned his mother. "That's strange," she said. "I've only seen that mind shifting gift among the Rhonnadon .... Where did you say the Karakan came from?"

Just then several large sand spiders scuttled out of the log Jonuke was leaning up against. Nya's eyes widened. "Duck, Jonuke!" She grabbed a large stick off the ground and used it like a bat to hit the spiders into the quicksand.

"Oh, no! I can't believe I just did that! Sand spiders and quicksand are best friends. It will allow them to multiply their numbers exponentially. Run! One bite will—"

"Turn you to sand," Jonuke finished as dozens of spiders swarmed after them. The two high-tailed it through the trees hoping to outrun them.

When Jonuke looked over his shoulder at the flood of spiders gaining on them, the Karakan's voice came into his head again. *Those spiders can't hurt you. They'll lead you to your mother. Go back.* Jonuke stopped in his tracks. He shook his head trying to clear his mind.

"Why are you stopping?" Nya shouted, running back for Jonuke. She knocked away the first wave of spiders with her stick, turning them to dust. "Safety is that way, remember?" She pointed over her shoulder.

She continued to fight the spiders but there were too many of them and Jonuke didn't seem to hear a word she said. She grabbed his hand and pulled him after her. Instantly, Jonuke was back to himself. "We need to have a serious talk, Vanguard," she said as they ran. "With your current state of mind, I have to say I'm a little worried about leaving Galvadon in your hands."

They burst through the trees and found themselves on the edge of a chasm. Jonuke shifted a blast that disintegrated the first wave of spiders but more took their place. "We're gonna have to jump," he shouted.

"Do you know how to fly?" Nya asked swatting away more spiders. "Because I sure don't."

"No," Jonuke replied, bodily grabbing Nya and diving over the edge of the cliff.

"Ahhh!" Nya shrieked as they plummeted downward. Jonuke put his fingers to his mouth and whistled.

"I can't fly, but he can." Sheezu swooped underneath the pair, catching them on his back. They watched the spiders spilling over the cliff's face as the screecher flew them up out of the abyss.

"That was close!" she sighed her relief. "And awesome! What a great way to start an adventure! Wait. You're friends with a screecher? Lucky!" she scratched Sheezu behind the ears. "I've never met a friendly one before."

"What are you doing?" Jonuke asked, when Nya gave Sheezu a big hug around the neck.

"What? He likes it," she said defensively. "Don't you? You're just a big kitty. Aren't you, aren't you?" she said rubbing his back. Then to Jonuke she said, "Actually, he wonders why you don't scratch him behind the ears. Ever. Not once, nada ... his words, not mine."

"Because we respect each other," answered Jonuke.

"Well, he says he would appreciate a little less respect and a little more belly scratchin'," Nya said patting Sheezu.

"So, if you're so good at communicating with animals, why didn't you have a talk with those spiders back there?" Jonuke challenged.

"Animals are like people," Nya explained. "Some you hit it off with right away and others, not so much. The spiders were feeling pretty grouchy about us waking them up from their nap and wouldn't listen to reason. You can't really blame them.

"And while we're asking questions of one another, what's up with the whole zombie act? You've got to learn to steel your mind against the Karakan's attacks.

"The only way to beat a mind shifter is to keep him out of your head," she continued. "Stop him at the first thought. He can't influence you if you don't let him. The mind shifters that I know use their abilities to help people. Instead of using fear, they use their gift to allow people to experience great adventures without having to leave home or risk their safety. Many have overcome fear of heights and other their crippling inhibitions.

"As soon as you hear him in your head. Say, 'No. I'm not listening to that' and replace the thought with one of your own. Let's practice. Pretend I'm the Karakan."

Nya cleared her throat and spoke in the deepest man voice she could manage. "Hey, Jonuke, why don't you jump in this quicksand over here? Don't worry, it's only water." She looked at Jonuke expectantly. "Your turn."

"What do you want me to say?" he asked awkwardly.

"Just like I said, 'No. I'm not listening to that.' Let's start again, but this time I'll work through your fears like he would." She lowered her voice, "Jonuke, I have your mother. You should be afraid, very afraid."

"No. I'm not listening to that," Jonuke parroted.

"With more feeling, if you really want to block him," Nya coached.

"No," Jonuke said definitively. "I'm not listening to that."

"Good! And?" she prompted.

"You won't have my mother for long. I'm coming for her as we speak."

"And a real clincher would be 'I'm the Vanguard and your days are numbered, buddy.' But that last part is totally optional," she smiled. "I just thought it sounded good."

Jonuke and Nya laughed together and brainstormed different come backs to block the Karakan's thoughts in Jonuke's head. Jonuke was glad he had met Nya.

*****

"Argh! Who is that girl?" the Karakan raged. "What is she doing? How does she know how to block a mind shifter? Well, whoever she is, she's ruining my game and has to be stopped."

*****

"We have to get back to Galvadon," Nya declared. "That's where the crown is."

"We?" Jonuke asked. "Isn't it against the rules for you to leave the Rhonnadon?"

"Hey, don't forget who saved your bacon back there. Twice."

"I just don't want you to get hurt," Jonuke reasoned.

"And I don't want you to get hurt either, but you don't see me telling you not to go," Nya replied.

"What do you think, Sheezu?" Jonuke asked his loyal companion. "Should we let her come?" The screecher walked over to Nya and nudged her onto his back. "Okay, it looks like I'm outnumbered," Jonuke observed, "but if there's trouble, promise me you'll get out of there and go home."

"Life is a risk, Jonuke," Nya replied, "and I'm your friend. Friends don't leave when the going gets tough. They have your back, and I have yours."

Sheezu flew Nya and Jonuke to the Citadel in no time at all. He dropped them off and then skulked off into the surrounding woodland hoping to find an afternoon snack. All was quiet.

"I was expecting you," the Karakan said, stepping out of the shadows. "I suppose you have come back for this?" He pointed to the crown on his head. "I've discovered that it is missing some very important parts, gems representing each of the nine kingdoms. Do you know where they are?" The Karakan probed Jonuke's mind for the answer.

You have let the crown and the sword slip through your fingers, Drek, and now I have them both. The Karakan's thoughts again forced their way in to his mind. *You will never defeat me!* Jonuke's mind started to fog.

"Don't let him in, Jonuke!" Nya warned.

Jonuke fought back with the techniques she had taught him. *No, I'm not listening to that. I hope you enjoyed your time with the crown and the sword because I'm taking them back.* Edging the Karakan out, his lucidity returned.

The Karakan was furious. He turned his wrath on Nya. "I have had enough of your meddling, Missy! Guards!" the Karakan ordered. The guards moved to secure Nya, but she was too quick and jabbed them both in the stomach with her elbow. However, a third came at her from behind and bound her wrists.

"Ah," the Karakan said to Jonuke as he looked into his mind. "You care for this one. Your fear for her safety has given away the fact that you have the gems with you in that pouch at your waist. Let me have them or your friend here will pay the price." Nya looked at Jonuke apologetically as he emptied the gems into the Karakan's hand.

"You are weak just like that Mahlneer fellow, allowing people to get in the way of what matters most: power. That is why you have failed, Drek, and *I* will be the greatest ruler Galvadon has ever known. Prophecy or no prophecy."

The Karakan held the crown over the gems. The jewels floated into the air and swirled around the crown embedding themselves one by one in the golden band. The Karakan smiled at his newest symbol of power. As he examined the crown, his brow furrowed at the sight of a missing gem. There was star-shaped indentation without its corresponding gem. "There's one missing. Where is the star-shaped gem, Drek?"

"I don't know. I haven't found it yet," Jonuke replied truthfully.

"I don't believe you. Tell me or you will never see this girl again." The Karakan pulled a long obsidian-handled paintbrush out of his inner vest pocket. Jonuke didn't know what the brush did but it couldn't be good. He decided it was time for this power monger to be taken down a notch.

Jonuke blasted the guard holding Nya and he fell back. "Oh, ho?! So you think you can defy me, Drek?" The Karakan drew the Master's Blade from its scabbard and nodded at the nearest guard to secure Nya before she could get away.

Jonuke tried to shift the sword out of the Karakan's hands but the sword repelled his attack knocking him backward. The Karakan laughed. "Behold the great Vanguard in all his glory. No one can stand against the power of the Blade, not even the Vanguard. Many have tried and all have failed."

Jonuke stood and tried again. He shifted a lightning strike at the sword but it was reflected back at him. Jonuke had to shift a shield to defend against his own attack.

"You've been practicing," the Karakan noted. "Your skills are impressive, but you can't defeat me. I hold an unconquerable sword. With it I have seized nearly all nine kingdoms. And you have given me the key to the others. They are being taken as we speak.

"Now watch as your friend here joins all the others who have defied me." The Karakan took a step toward Nya with the paintbrush extended. Jonuke dove protectively in front of her and as soon as the brush touched him, he started to disappear.

"Ha! You will now join my living mural and I will have all sorts of fun with you. And you'll just have to wonder what happens to your girlfriend without you here to protect her."

"Actually, I won't." Jonuke put his fingers to his mouth and whistled loudly. "Sheez, take her home!" he shouted. Just before he disappeared, he saw a black blur carrying Nya off into the horizon.

"You'll pay for that little trick, Drek. You'll pay," the Karakan said spitefully. "No one defies the Karakan and gets away with it."

CHAPTER 19

It's a Small World

The Karakan stood at the mural in the council room and searched for its newest addition, the Vanguard. "Let's see what you're really made of, Vanguard." With a few flicks of his brush he added a swarm of hornets to the painting just above Jonuke. "Now that my Vanguard problem has been handled, I'm off to conquer the fairies," he said. The Karakan held out a feather that matched the one he had given Silvane and swirled it in the air. He stepped into the portal he had just created and disappeared.

*****

"The fairy kingdom is up there, Great Karakan," Silvane pointed to a small door near a great waterfall. "Some of my men traveled here with Scithe in pursuit of the Lawbreakers. We found it again easily." He handed the feather back to the Karakan.

"Good work, General," the Karakan replied tucking the feathers away inside his vest.

*****

"My lady, there are intruders in our land," the fairy captain reported to the queen.

"Gather your men and chase them out again," she replied tartly.

"I'm afraid that won't be very easy," the captain started.

"Easy? Is that how the captain of my guard lives his life—based upon whether something is 'easy' or not? I highly doubt that is how you received your recommendation for captain," she sniffed.

"These are no simple explorers. These men are here to conquer the Fairy Kingdom," the captain tried to explain to his prideful leader.

"What?! How dare they?!" the queen shouted. "This is *my* kingdom and I will not tolerate attempts to usurp the throne! Arm your fairies with the poison darts."

"As you wish, my queen," the captain bowed and flitted out of the room

Dozens of fairies lined up in their ranks, prepared for battle. The fairy queen headed the soldiers. The Karakan stood in front of his small squad of Elite. "Fairy queen," he said boldly, "a new age has begun in Galvadon. You are my subjects now."

"You don't own me and you have no idea with whom you are dealing. No one enters the Fairy Kingdom uninvited. Attack!" she ordered.

The fairies advanced and put their blow guns to their mouths. "Fire!" ordered the captain. The fairies released dozens of small arrows at the invaders.

The Karakan held up the Master's Blade and the arrows turned and flew back at the fairies. Almost every fairy was hit with an arrow. Luckily for them, they each carried a vial of antidote for the poison and revived quickly.

The stubborn queen ordered another volley of darts with the same effect. The fairy captain flitted over to the queen and whispered, "We carry but two doses of the antidote. If we try another attack, we will lose many fairies. The sword he holds cannot be defeated with our darts. We must surrender."

The fairy queen stamped her foot and folded her arms across her chest. She hated losing. "We surrender. Fairies, throw down your weapons." The fairies followed the queen's order and the Terran Elite fashioned small cages to carry the fairies back to Galvadon.

"Excellent, General Silvane!" said the Karakan thoroughly enjoying his victory. "And on the way home, let's conquer Palean. I'll have two additions to my mural before nightfall."

*****

"Sheezu! Take me back to the Citadel!" Nya demanded. Sheezu maintained a steady course for the castle. "I know Jonuke told you to take me home. He was trying to protect me, but he needs our help. The Karakan has Jonuke. With the Vanguard gone, who will save Galvadon?" But Sheezu wouldn't listen. Although he liked Nya, he was loyal to Jonuke first. Sheezu's ears perked up at the sight of to two screechers circling above the treetops in the distance.

"You know you want to go and see what they've found over there," Nya tempted. She saw Sheezu looking at the screechers longingly. "Let's just go take a quick look and then you can take me home." This time, Sheezu was persuaded.

After all, he was still taking her home like Jonuke had said. He was just taking a small detour on the way. Sheezu kept his distance, not wanting the other screechers to feel their prey was being poached. He just wanted to see what had them so excited. But it was Nya that saw them first, a woman and a girl running for their lives through the trees.

"What do you mean it's their kill?" Nya said. "Jonuke wouldn't let you get away with an excuse like that and you know it. We need to help them." Grudgingly Sheezu agreed and landed in front of the girls.

At the sight of an enormous screecher, they shrieked and ran the other way. Nya leapt down from Sheezu's back "Wait!" she yelled as the girls disappeared into the trees. "He's friendly!" she said racing after them. The good news was Nya caught up with them easily. The bad news was so did one of the other screechers.

The girls backed up slowly toward Nya as the screecher snarled and took a step closer. "Let me handle this," Nya said stepping out in front of the girls. She held out her hand as a sign of peace to the drooling beast.

"Hi, my name's Nya," she started, hoping to be able to reason with the screecher. "Yes, I know you're hungry. You actually have a little drool leaking out of this side of your mouth there—" Her hand went to her mouth to indicate the location of the drool.

The spit dripped to the ground and the animal growled. "Okay, so you don't have much of a sense of humor. That's okay. So, these two ladies behind me are mostly skin and bone. Not much of a meal for a big guy like you." She paused for a moment listening. "Oh, so they're just a snack to tide you over 'til dinner? Well, in that case ...." she trailed off unable to argue with his logic. "No, no, no. That's a terrible idea. You need to go find another midday snack. Now, go! Shew!" she commanded waving her hands at the creature.

The screecher hissed and sprang at Nya but was intercepted by Sheezu. He pinned the attacker to the ground and snarled. Just then, the screecher's hunting partner leapt out from the trees and pounced on Sheezu. Sheezu roared and swiped back.

It wasn't a fair fight, two against one. However, Sheezu was quite a bit larger than the others and held his own. This wasn't his first fight and he clawed and bit until the screechers changed their minds about being hungry. The two flew away as quickly as their wings would take them.

Sheezu walked over to Nya and checked her for injuries. "I'm fine. I'm the one that should be giving you the checkup," she giggled when his whiskers brushed past her neck.

"I don't think he's pleased with you for helping us," the woman said. "He thinks you should be at home, not here."

"That's exactly what he said," Nya marveled. "How did you know that?"

"It is a gift my people are born with."

"To read minds?" Nya guessed.

"No, to mimic the gifts of others. You must have the gift of communicating with animals?

"That is exactly right! Are you sure you can't read minds?" Nya asked.

"No, like I said my gift is to replicate other's gifts. When I discovered I had the ability to understand your screecher friend there, I assumed it was because you also had that ability. And now it seems he is in quite a rush to get you home."

"Sheezu, don't be so rude," Nya scolded. "We haven't even been properly introduced to these ladies." She held out her hand. "Hi, I'm Nya and this is my friend Sheezu. We were flying overhead and saw you were in trouble."

"I'm M'lai and this is my daughter Iliana and we are very grateful for your help. Thank you Sheezu for letting Nya stop and for fighting those screechers for us. We are in your debt." Sheezu grunted his acceptance of her thanks.

"So can we give you a lift home?" Nya offered.

"Our home is Galvadon and that isn't a safe place for us right now," said M'lai.

"Galvadon?" Nya asked. "But I thought you said you were mimics. Where are the rest of your people?"

"Gone. Wiped out by a sickness, sipro fever, that mimics are more susceptible to than most. Iliana and I are the last of our kind." M'lai told Nya about her life in

Galvadon with Silvane, about her children Scithe and Iliana, how they had runaway to Aeris, and that they were now hiding in the Darke Forest from her husband.

"Our home is Galvadon, but we have met some nice Drek that have watched over us since we've been here. They told us not to go far, but we were berry picking and didn't realize how far we'd gone. That's when we saw the screechers circling," M'lai explained.

"M'lai? Iliana?" came a man's voice through the trees. A tall man with broad shoulders and dark hair came upon the little group. "M'lai! Iliana! We saw the screechers and came running. Are you alright?"

"We are thanks to Nya and Sheezu," M'lai said indicating her two new friends.

"Sheezu?! What are you doing here? Where's Jonuke?" the man asked.

It was Nya's turn to be surprised. "You know Jonuke?"

"Know him? He's my son," Londor replied.

CHAPTER 20

In the Mural

Jonuke dove into a bush as a hornet the size of a horse buzzed by. He peeked out from between the leaves, saw the coast was clear, but waited until he was sure. He watched as the hornet rejoined its swarm and identified a new target.

Jonuke climbed out of the bush and wondered where they were headed. He followed the swarm, keeping a safe distance. He found the hornets hovering just above the surface of a pond. And then he saw what they were after, a boy about Jonuke's age burst out of the water and gasp for air.

The boy tried to dive back under the water before the hornet got him but the insects were quicker than he, and he was stung. The boy lost consciousness and floated to the top of the pond. The hornets began stinging the easy target repeatedly.

"Stop!" Jonuke yelled sending lightning bolts from the sky. The hornets speedily buzzed away with singed wings. Jonuke dove into the water and retrieved the still form. He pulled him out of the water and onto the shore. The boy had swollen up like a balloon and wasn't breathing. Jonuke knew he had only minutes before the boy suffocated.

Jonuke let his hands hover over the boy's body as he assessed his wounds until he located the highest concentrations of poison. There was a lot in his system but Jonuke felt he could safely help him. Jonuke didn't feel that it was the boy's time to go.

Jonuke visualized the venom and reversed its path back up and out of the sting sites. The yellow poison pooled out of the boy's body and dripped onto the ground. With the poison gone, Jonuke could focus on the anaphylaxis. He drew the excess fluid out of the sweat glands until the swelling was reduced considerably.

The boy gasped for breath and doubled over. "Ahh! What just happened to me?"

"You were attacked by the largest hornets I've ever seen," Jonuke replied.

"I remember that part, but how am I still alive?" He looked at Jonuke's wet clothing and surmised that he had rescued him. "You?" he asked. Jonuke nodded. "Thanks," the boy said holding out his hand. "The name is Flynn."

"Jonuke." And the boys clasped hands.

"Wait a minute … I know you. You're that Drek that had the funky test. The Karakan had to stop it because all the screechers gave up and flew away. That never happens. That was awesome, man! Never seen anything like it. So when did you learn that you could shift?" Jonuke was taken aback by the question. He thought Flynn had been unconscious during the fireworks.

"Yeah, I saw the lightning right before I passed out. That was also awesome by the way. What Element was that?"

"I am an Energy shifter," Jonuke replied. He had no problem sharing his identity now that the Karakan knew who he was.

"Can't say I've ever heard that one before, but to each his own, dude. So whatcha in here for? Did you 'disappoint,'" Flynn paused to emphasize the air quotes, "the Karakan, too? I was supposed to bring in the Supreme Council to earn the title of captain on an Elite squad. Clearly that didn't happen.

"I tried to act like the Elite, but it just wasn't me, bro. The Karakan wasn't happy, so he painted me in here and sicked a screecher on me. Have to say, I prefer all that's happened to me in here to being an Elite and chasing Granny all over Galvadon."

"Wait, you went up against Granny?" Jonuke asked.

"Yes, and she made me regret it," Flynn chuckled. "In here I can just be myself. How about you? What did you do anyway?"

"Well, the Karakan found out that I'm the Vanguard that's supposed to rule Galvadon and he didn't like that too much. I attempted to take away his sword, and when he tried to paint my friend I got in the way. I think the hornets were meant for me. Sorry about that," Jonuke apologized.

"No worries," Flynn replied. "Just another day in the Darke Forest, but the Vanguard? That's intense, man."

"Yes, very intense," Jonuke agreed. "So you've been in here longer than I have. Any idea how we're going to get out of here?"

"No, this place is just miles and miles of forest. No way out that I know of," Flynn replied.

Jonuke looked around him. Other than the fact that he and everything around him was now two dimensional, it was an exact replica of the Darke Forest. He recognized the trees and this particular pond. He knew right where he was. "Do you know where this painting is located in the real world?"

"Yeah. It's in the Citadel in the old council room," Flynn replied. Jonuke nodded. He recalled seeing the mural of the Darke Forest.

"Maybe if we can find the Citadel in the painting, we can find a way out," Jonuke suggested.

"Everyone will be happy to hear that," Flynn said.

"Everyone?" Jonuke asked.

"Yeah, the Karakan's painted a lot of people in here," Flynn replied.

"Do you know where they all are?" Jonuke asked.

"Sure. Finding them isn't the problem," said Flynn.

*****

Flynn led Jonuke to the top of a hill. "Look down there," Flynn pointed to an older-looking man standing amongst the trees with his arms outstretched to the sky. He wasn't moving, just standing there.

"What's wrong with him?" Jonuke asked.

"The dude thinks he's a tree," explained Flynn.

"How do you know that?" asked Jonuke.

"Go see for yourself," Flynn said.

Jonuke walked down the hill and approached the man. "Hello, my name is Jonuke and we're looking for a way out of this painting. Would you like to come with us?"

"If only I wasn't a tree," the man said, "I would introduce myself. I'd say something like 'Hi, I'm Raef, leader of the elves.' I'd tell this young man that I would love to come with him, but alas, I am rooted to the ground and cannot go."

"You're not a tree," Jonuke reasoned.

"It won't work," Flynn called down from the hill. He'd found a fruit tree and was munching on something crunchy.

"I wish this boy, Jonuke, were a tree and then I would have some company," Raef mourned. The man's lament had given Jonuke an idea. He planted his feet on the ground next to the man and held his arms up in the air.

"What are you doing?" asked Flynn.

"If only that Aerisian could speak the language of the trees," Jonuke said sadly, "I'd tell him to quit yelling so loudly and to chew with his mouth closed."

"He's lost it," Flynn muttered.

But Raef suddenly perked up. "Oh, another tree! I've been so lonely. How did you come to be here?"

"Painted in. Karakan found out I'm the Vanguard," answered Jonuke.

"You're the Vanguard?!" said Raef excitedly. "You can help my people. The Karakan captured them and painted me in here."

Jonuke suddenly looked alarmed. "Oh, what's happening?!" he exclaimed. "I *can* move my branches. No, my *arms*! My branches have turned back into arms! I can't believe it. And my legs! I can move them! Look, Raef! You, too! Look at your arms!"

Raef looked up and was surprised to discover arms, not branches and feet, not roots. "I'm an elf again," he rejoiced.

"Will you come with us?" Jonuke asked. "We are looking for the other people trapped in here."

"Yes, I will gladly come. There was a dwarf making quite a racket not far from here," Raef explained leading the way.

"You're a genius, Jonuke. A genius," said Flynn as he ran to catch up to them.

Raef was right. They found the dwarf in the next clearing swearing up a storm. "How am I supposed to compete with those when all I have is gravel for materials?" The dwarf gestured angrily at several high pillars surrounding him. He was struggling to construct one taller but his only materials were a handful of pebbles. No matter how he arranged them, he couldn't make his tower taller than the competition.

When Jonuke approached him and asked if he would come with them, and he adamantly refused. He wasn't going anywhere until he had the tallest tower. His eyes were blood shot and red. He hadn't slept since he'd gotten here.

"If we can help you build the tallest tower, will you come with us?" Jonuke asked and the dwarf agreed.

"How are we going to do that?" Flynn asked. "There aren't any big rocks around here, just these pebbles he's been using."

"Watch and learn, Flynn," Jonuke winked rolling up his sleeves.

"Alright!" Flynn clapped his hands in anticipation. "Let's see what an Energy shifter can do!"

Jonuke focused on the columns and held his hands out in front of him. The pillars began to vibrate and then shake violently. "Everybody get back," Jonuke shouted and they took shelter just before the towers exploded. Jonuke stepped out and levitated the rocks one on top of the other and then fused them all together into a towering column.

"It's magnificent," the dwarf gasped. "I'll remember this tower 'til the day I die. Just one more thing before we go. The dwarf rushed over to the base of the tower and wrote in the dirt. "Bilhard's Tower."

"There, I claimed it. It's mine. Let's go."

Just then Truen, Scithe and Yondel emerged through the trees. "What's all this racket about over here? Jonuke?" they said in unison. Truen grabbed

Jonuke and gave him a bone crunching hug. "It's been a long time, Vanguard."

"Too long," Jonuke agreed slapping him on the back. "I'd like you Truen, Yondel and Scithe to meet our fellow prisoners Bilhard, Raef and Flynn."

"Raef and I have met," Truen nodded in recognition.

"Any word from Taeliah?" Raef asked and Truen shook his head.

Scithe looked at Flynn who was smoldering in silence. Scithe walked over to him and held out a hand in greeting. "Didn't we compete in the—" Scithe started but instead of shaking his hand, Flynn punched him in the face.

"That was for the Games," Flynn growled.

Truen laughed out loud as Scithe rubbed his sore jaw. "So are we good?" Scithe asked.

"Yeah we're good," Flynn replied and then punched him in the gut.

"Oh, ho!" Truen guffawed. "That one had to hurt."

"It did," Scithe wheezed. "I thought you said we were good, Flynn."

"We are. That was for my buddy, Aerik," Flynn replied rubbing his sore knuckles.

Scithe took a moment to catch his breath. "So now are we good?" he asked.

Flynn nodded. "We're good."

"*All* good?" Scithe asked.

"All good," Flynn smirked.

Jonuke and the others rounded up the remaining rulers: the Sage of the gnomes, Wardek of the Wolves, Grog of the giants, the queen of the fairies, and Daelik of Palean. Some came more readily like the Sage, Grog and Daelik, but the queen of the fairies and Wardek took some convincing. By the time Jonuke had helped them out of whatever difficulty the Karakan had painted them into, their respect for him had grown and they were looking to him to find a way out of the painting.

"I think our best chance to get out of here is to find a way out the forest and back to the Citadel," Jonuke suggested.

"Already tried that," Yondel replied. "The edges of the forest are just painted trees. We've walked the perimeter of this entire painting and there is no way out that we've been able to find."

Just then Bilhard gasped. "What-is-*that*?" He pointed to a tall grey tower, much taller than the one Jonuke had just built for him. A murmur broke out amongst the rulers. They'd never seen that tower there before.

Jonuke recognized the tower immediately as the one from his dream. He looked down at locket that he wore around his neck. It was glowing.

CHAPTER 21

How it all Began

Without taking the time to explain, Jonuke sprinted through the trees toward the tower. Branches scratched and slapped against his face, but he didn't care. He ignored the shouts of his friends behind him and ran as fast as his legs would carry him. As he neared the tower he could hear a faint singing coming from the single window at the top of the tower.

There was a door at the base of the tower but it was locked. Jonuke's grabbed the handle. His eyes glowed silver as energy surged down his arm into the door and blew it off its hinges. Jonuke stepped over the twisted door and raced up the stairs. The woman standing at the window singing hadn't heard Jonuke come in. Her song was one he'd heard many times before in the moments just before he fell asleep.

"Mom?" Jonuke called out in little more than a whisper.

Linayah whirled around, surprised to hear her name. "Jonuke?" She was afraid to believe that her son was actually standing in the same room with her. "You found me? Are you really here?" she asked as he approached her. "Or am I dreaming again?"

"I'm really here," Jonuke reassured. "I'd like to give you a hug. Is it alright if I touch you?" he asked tentatively, remembering the disastrous consequences the last time they touched.

"Of course it is, honey!" She held out her arms and they embraced. "How I've missed you!" They hugged for a long while enjoying being together after such a long separation. "But if you're here, that means ...?"

"I'm in the painting, but I'll get us out. I'll find a way," Jonuke promised. "So, this is where you've been all these years?" he asked. "Locked away in this tower?" Linayah nodded sadly. "But why? Why would the Karakan do this to you?"

Linayah sat down in the window seat and gestured for Jonuke to join her. "It all began when my brother Dendrid and I decided to break the rules. I've since come to regret that decision, sorely. But then if I hadn't, I wouldn't have you, would I?" she smiled at Jonuke and caressed his cheek.

"I'm getting ahead of myself. By now you must know that I am a Rhonnadon," Linayah started. Jonuke nodded. "What you might not have discovered yet is that I have a brother, Dendrid, but you know him better as the Karakan."

"The Karakan is your brother? My uncle?" Jonuke let that information sink in for a moment. "Your brother, my uncle, did this to you, to us?" he asked in disbelief.

Linayah nodded sadly. "Long ago when the Rhonnadon dwelt in Galvadon, it was a time of great peace and prosperity. When the time came that the people no longer desired their leadership, the Rhonnadon left. My people still feel a great sadness at being separated from Galvadon. We love your people....

"My brother and I had never known Galvadon and greatly desired to see it. We had been raised among the Rhonnadon and been taught our history. The Elementals fascinated us and piqued our curiosity. After all, could the animosity between the cities really be that bad? Why did the Rhonnadon have to leave?

"We wanted to see Galvadon, the city we had grown up hearing about, the city that had been prophesied to which we would one day return, but it was strictly forbidden. The Rhonnadon would not return to Galvadon until one of its people sought us out and they were ready to live in peace.

"'But how would they find us?' we reasoned. We had been gone for so long, would they even remember the Rhonnadon existed?

"Dendrid and I discussed this topic at length. One day he suggested that we go to Galvadon to see it for ourselves. I adamantly refused. It was against the rules the Elders had made, and I knew there had to be a good reason for those rules. But Dendrid continued to talk with me about the wonders of Galvadon. Wasn't I just a little curious? We could just take a look and then come right back home.

"I knew he was angry about being passed over to learn the tongue of Rhonnadon. My father saw his thirst for power and didn't trust Dendrid. I should have known that he had ulterior motives for seeking out Galvadon, but I didn't. His arguments were very persuasive and I eventually agreed. It sounded like a grand adventure after all.

"When we arrived in Galvadon, it was more than we hoped it would be. We were amazed at the skill the Elementals had with shifting the Elements and with what they had built for themselves. However, there were also things that were disturbing about Galvadon. The heated contention between the cities, the fighting and frequent battles, and most of all, the Drek. The people who had been cast out of Galvadon for not having an Elemental gift.

"At this point, I had seen enough and told Dendrid it was time to go home, but he wasn't ready to leave. He said he wanted to 'help' Galvadon. He wanted to use his mind shifting abilities to persuade Galvadon to adopt the ways of the Rhonnadon so they could get along. He said we could rule Galvadon together, but I didn't want any part of that. He called me selfish for not wanting to share our knowledge of peace with them. But I wasn't selfish, this wasn't the way of the Rhonnadon.

"It was then that Dendrid's true intent became clear. He had never planned to return to the Rhonnadon. I insisted that we return home, that it was not our way use trickery to gain power. He refused. After our argument, we parted ways. I intended to return home, but when traveling through the Darke Forest, I had a bit of bad luck. I hurt my ankle and it wasn't long before the night hunters began closing in.

"Lucky for me, your father was close by and heard my calls for help. He fought the creatures off single-handedly and took me back to his home to assess my injured ankle. He asked why I was traveling so late. Didn't I know that it wasn't safe at night in the Darke Forest?

"Londor wrapped my ankle and allowed me to stay with him while it healed. You know your father, the first day he built me a pair of crutches so I wouldn't be confined to the house. Once I was mobile, he had me exploring the forest with him. In one week's time, I knew all there was to know about the Darke Forest: names of plants and animals, tips and tricks for survival, how to identify edible plants, and how to find my way back to the house blindfolded!" she laughed at the memory.

"It wasn't long before Londor and I realized we were in love and were married. I had long since told him about my home with the Rhonnadon and that I had decided to stay. Not long after we were married, you came along, Jonuke. I'd never seen your father so happy as the day you were born.

"We lived a quiet life, a beautiful life. It was perfect, but it wouldn't last. While I was living the quiet life in the forest, Dendrid had been busy. He had first convinced himself that he was the fulfillment of the ancient prophecy and that he was the rightful ruler of Galvadon and then set about to convince the Elementals.

"Some resisted his rule, so he organized the Supreme Council to assuage the resistance. He still feared the prophecy and knew that one day the Vanguard could emerge and take Galvadon away from him. In order to do this, the Vanguard would need to bring the Rhonnadon home to Galvadon, so he prohibited all travel beyond the Darke Forest.

"Then, he turned his sights on the Drek. He didn't like that these people were independent of his reign and so he flattered the Council into accepting his proposal of Drek servitude.

"I knew what my brother was doing in Galvadon and I didn't like it, but I tried to ignore it. After all, it didn't affect me and my family. We were safe in our own little world in the forest. The Elementals up to this point had left us alone because of the dangers posed by the Darke Forest.

"When I learned that Dendrid meant to enslave the Drek, my little world shattered. I couldn't let him do that to my family. I couldn't let my sweet innocent boy grow up as a servant. Without telling Londor, I snuck away one night and confronted my brother. He was surprised to see me for he had believed that I had gone home to the Rhonnadon. I told him what he was doing in Galvadon wasn't our way. It wasn't right.

"Dendrid didn't care about my opinion of him. He was having too much fun playing his little game as ruler of Galvadon. I tried to reason with him, to talk sense into him, to help him see how he was hurting the Drek. He argued that he had brought peace to Galvadon, that the warring had stopped. I demanded that he leave the Drek alone, but he just laughed at me.

"I tried to help him remember the ways of the Rhonnadon. They wouldn't want this. What would our father think if he knew what Dendrid was up to? He didn't like hearing that. He said I was threatening him. He thought that I meant to return to the Rhonnadon and tattle on him. And the next thing I knew, I was in this tower."

All that his mother had told him was a lot to process. After a long pause, Jonuke asked, "If you were in this tower all these years, how have you been able to visit me?"

"Although my gift is that of a healer, I have developed other abilities. Many of the Rhonnadon have. Dendrid was always jealous of my aptitude for picking up new skills quickly. I could sense when you were in danger or lonely and could visit you in your dreams at these times. But when your gifts became stronger, I realized I had the ability to visit you when you were fully awake, like that fateful day in the cave not long ago. I shouldn't have stayed. I knew Dendrid could sense that I had left. When you touched me, he was able to discern exactly where I was. If only I had healed you and left, he wouldn't have found us and you wouldn't be trapped in here right now."

"And if I wasn't in here, I wouldn't have found you. Everything happens for a reason, Mother. We'll find a way out of here," Jonuke reassured. He thought for a moment and then asked, "I understand the servitude part, but why does the Karakan test the Drek?"

"Because Dendrid is a Rhonnadon, he understood more about the prophecy than the Elementals who had largely forgotten about it or discounted it as a fable. Dendrid knew the Vanguard would be one of our own bloodline, one of pure Rhonnadonian descent. It was then that he devised the plan to stop the Vanguard before he discovered who he was.

"He decided to test the Drek using their greatest fears against them, further convincing them that they had no gift. If one did produce an unusual talent, he would identify him as the Vanguard and dispose of him before he knew it himself. The Vanguard would come and go without ever knowing the power he had within.

"I don't understand," Jonuke said. "He was looking for a pureblood Rhonnadon. What does this have to do with the Drek?"

"There are no Drek," Linayah replied.

"What?" asked Jonuke. His head was beginning to reel with all of the new information.

"The people you call Drek are actually a remnant of the Rhonnadon who, over time, have forgotten who they are. Without the written histories of my people, their true past was lost. For the Rhonnadon, gifts do not manifest as easily as the Elementals. They have to really work to develop them. We have those among us called 'discerners' who can identify one's gift before it is developed so they know where to focus their efforts. Believing you have a gift is the first step. Because of the special role you have to play in life, Jonuke, you are an exception to that rule."

"Wait, so you're saying all the Drek have gifts and they just haven't discovered them yet?" Jonuke said trying to process the implications of this new information.

"Much was lost to your people when the Rhonnadon left," Linayah explained.

"Wasn't it difficult living with my father with that secret? Without telling him that he had a gift?" Jonuke asked.

"There were no secrets between me and your father. He knew. Without a discerner it was difficult to define his gift, but eventually we figured it out."

"You did?" Jonuke couldn't believe what he was hearing.

"Have you ever noticed how your dad has an uncanny ability to know when things are about to happen? He calls it a sixth sense." Jonuke nodded. "We discovered that he is a discerner."

"But why didn't he tell me? Why didn't he tell the rest of the Drek about their gifts?"

"Your father's gift told him you were the Vanguard. It was then that I placed the shield over the Darke Forest so that your identity would remain hidden from Dendrid. Londor didn't share his knowledge about gifts with the Drek, because his first duty was to you, to protect you until you were old enough to learn who you were. He didn't want to attract the Karakan's attention to his young son. And he didn't tell you about his abilities because you weren't ready yet."

Just then Yondel's head poked into the room. "Jonuke?" she said. Jonuke beckoned her over to them. "Everyone is worried about you. Are you alright?"

"Never better. Yondel, meet my mother Linayah."

CHAPTER 22

Getting Out

"How is it that you ended up with his pet screecher?" Londor asked. Nya explained how she and Jonuke had met in the Forgotten Kingdom. "You're a Rhonnadon? He found the Rhonnadon ...?" Londor asked in hushed tones.

Nya blushed and nodded and continued her story. She told about the Karakan taking the crown and gems and how Jonuke had protected her form the Karakan and how Sheezu had brought her here.

"Well done, Sheezu! And you, Nya. Though you downplayed it, it sounds like you helped Jonuke out of a pickle more than once." Nya blushed again. She really liked Londor. He was very kind.

"I have so many questions for you all," said Londor. "Let's get back to the house where it's safe." He sent Sheezu off to do the hunting he was aching for and took the three girls back to his home. Renden was there and Londor filled him in on all he'd missed.

"Aren't we lucky you flew by, Nya?" Renden smiled. "The Karakan has been so busy conquering Galvadon and all the surrounding lands that he hasn't had time for the Drek," said Renden. "We've been able to go back to life as usual for now."

Renden cleaned off the table in preparation for their evening meal. The table was littered with quite a few wooden tubes. "Without our regular assignments to keep us busy, we have a lot of extra time on our hands. Londor and I have been carving these blow guns just to keep busy. Coupled with the sleep darts we've been collecting, I think we have enough to fight a small war. What do you think, Londor?"

Londor chuckled and agreed. He went to the cupboard and pulled out some dried meat and biscuits for his guests.

"The berries were going to be for dessert," Iliana lamented.

"Don't give it a second thought," Renden reassured her. "We're just glad you are safe."

Nya noticed Iliana was fidgeting with an odd-looking gem on her necklace. "That's an interesting looking necklace," said Nya.

"My mother gave it to me," Iliana smiled.

"It's a very special family heirloom passed down through the generations. We were told to always look after it because one day someone would come looking for it."

"May I see it?" Nya asked. Iliana removed the necklace and handed it to Nya. The gem was aquamarine and cut in the shape of a star, a star that exactly matched that of the missing gemstone on the Crown of Rulers.

While all this had been going on, Londor had become suddenly quiet. His gift of discernment sometimes triggered automatically and this was one of those times. He saw an epic battle unfolding. All of Galvadon was about to be destroyed, and Jonuke was in the middle of it. He saw Jonuke urging the people to stand together against the power of the Karakan, but even that wasn't enough. Then the vision closed.

"We need to get back to Galvadon," Londor and Nya said in unison.

"But first, let's rally the troops," Londor said gathering up the blow darts and ammo. "Jonuke needs our help."

*****

"From my tower, I once saw the paintbrush enter the painting," Linayah told Jonuke.

"Where was that?" he asked.

"Just above that mountain," she pointed to a distant peak. "I wonder if that might be a pathway to and from the painting."

Jonuke looked up at the giant, Grog. "It's a long walk for our short legs. Do you think you could get us there a little more quickly?"

Grog smiled a wide scraggle-toothed grin. "Yes, Son of Londor." He reached out and scooped up half the rulers with his right arm and then the other half with his left, holding them tightly under his arms.

"Let me out of this stinky armpit!" The fairy queen shrieked as she squeezed out of Grog's iron grip. "I can get there just fine on my own," she huffed as she smoothed her skirt.

Grog ran through the trees with great lumbering strides and had them to the top of the mountain in no time. He unceremoniously tossed the jostled crew onto the ground.

Truen rubbed his head. "That wasn't one of your better ideas, Jonuke," he noted. "But I guess it got the job done."

"He got us here quickly and that means we're that much closer to freedom," Wardek of Haldan countered. "Never mind his methods."

"I sense something different in the aura in this particular location of the forest," said the gnome Sage. "I believe we are near the doorway."

The Karakan who had just happened to be walking by the mural was alarmed by seeing all of his painted people standing together on top of this mountain. *What has that Drek done to my game? He's ruined everything! Let's see the Vanguard rescue them from this!* The Karakan pulled out his paintbrush and began vigorously painting.

The people in the painting watched as the paintbrush descended from above and touched the mountain. They heard the sounds of something, a lot of somethings, climbing toward them. Flynn took to the air and then shouted, "Jonuke, we've got a problem. The mountain is covered with giant scorpions and they are headed right for us."

Grog grabbed the first scorpion by the tail and swung it in circles over his head and sent it flying over the treetops. The warriors in the group sprang into action. Daelik, Bilhard, and Raef engaged in hand to claw combat with the critters while Wardek transformed into a wolf, fearlessly charged, and sank his teeth into the nearest scorpion's leg. Flynn blew several of the large insects off the mountainside while Scithe created sink pits that swallowed them whole. Jonuke blasted hordes of them with a sonic boom.

Truen and Yondel fought side by side, fire and ice at their best. She froze scuttling legs together while he incinerated them with fireballs. Out of the corner of his eye, Truen caught sight of an enemy just as its claw seized Yondel. Time seemed to stop as the poison barbed tail darted toward her.

"NO! Yondel!" he roared aware of a rage he didn't know he was capable of feeling. Summoning every part of himself into flame, he consumed the beast with a white wall of fire instantly turning every part of it to ash, every part but the claw that held Yondel. No longer attached to anything, it clattered to the ground lifelessly. Truen rushed over to Yondel and took her into his arms.

"Yondel, are you alright?" he asked anxiously.

Yondel threw her arms around his neck. "Thank you, Truen!" she exclaimed hugging him tightly.

"I'll always be there for you," he replied brushing a stray hair from her face. The two smiled at each other for a time saying nothing.

"Truen," started Yondel.

"Yeah," he replied.

"Now would be the perfect time to kiss me," she said smiling up at him.

Having all but given up on ever hearing those words, a look of surprise flashed across his eyes. But the momentary hesitation passed quickly, and Truen kissed Yondel.

Somewhat stunned, Yondel exclaimed, "Wow! So what took you so long to do that?!"

"What took *me* so long?" Truen coughed in comical disbelief.

"It's about time you two got together!" Jonuke shouted running toward them.

Truen and Yondel sprang back into action fighting with everything they had. All in the group did what they could to fight the swarm of numberless scorpions, but they couldn't protect everyone, and Bilhard was stung.

Linayah rushed to his side and did what she could to ease the pain and remove the venom. "We can't hold them off forever. Whenever you clear some away, Dendrid paints more in their place. We can't fight them as quickly as he can paint them. I can heal Bilhard, but what happens when multiple people are injured? It's a battle we can't win."

Jonuke knew she was right. He watched the Karakan's brush as it painted more scorpions. *If the brush brought them in here*, he thought, *why couldn't it bring them out again?* "Grog!" Jonuke shouted. The giant flung a scorpion and then lumbered over to Jonuke. "Do you think you could grab ahold of that paintbrush the next time you see it?

Grog flexed his strong looking hands. "Grog the giant can, Son of Londor," he boomed.

"Good. The next time you see the Karakan's paint-brush grab it and don't let go." They didn't have long to wait. The warriors had cleared another layer of scorpions and the Karakan began to paint more. As soon as the paintbrush appeared, Grog grasped the bristles.

"It's time to go!" Jonuke shouted. "Everyone grab onto Grog. The train is leaving the station."

As the Karakan, started to withdraw the brush, Grog clung to it and was lifted off the mountain top. Everyone found a strap, leg, or toe to grab onto and they were lifted up and out of the painting.

CHAPTER 23

Epic Battle

The Karakan watched in bewilderment as everyone he had ever painted into the mural came out again. He couldn't believe what he was seeing. *How had they gotten out of the painting? It wasn't possible!*

"How could you?!" Linayah said storming over to Dendrid. "How could you take me from my family?"

"You were always weak, Linayah," he replied. "You could have ruled Galvadon with me."

"It was never our right to do so. That right lies with my son, Jonuke, the Vanguard and true ruler of Galvadon." Linayah yanked the paintbrush out of her brother's hand and broke it in half. As soon as she did so the wall containing the mural crumbled to the ground.

Unfortunately, that wall was the Citadel's primary load bearing wall and the ceiling started to collapse. Grog held up the roof up until everyone could get out of the building and then let it collapse. All the people from the city came out of their homes and looked in amazement at the huge cloud of dust and debris. The Elite, suddenly on high alert, rushed to the top of the hill to await their orders and Galvadon's confused citizens followed in their wake. When the dust settled, all that remained of the Citadel was a small section of the mural.

"It's over Dendrid," said Jonuke. "The people of Galvadon don't want you here."

"You, a common Drek, speak as if you are the voice of Galvadon," the Karakan scoffed.

The members of the Supreme Council separated themselves from the crowd. "He speaks for Hydra," shouted Oregg. "And Pyros, and Aeris, and Terra," the others added.

"We follow the Vanguard," declared Raef, the leader of the elves. The rulers of each of the kingdoms stood next to Raef indicating their agreement to what he had just said. The fairy queen hesitated for just a moment, but the peer pressure got to her and she joined the others.

"How dare you defy me?!" the Karakan raged. "You will all kneel at my feet before the sun sets on this day! Silvane, show Galvadon who their true ruler is."

"Unleash the Elements!" the general shouted. At Silvane's command four squads of Elite spread out and shifted the most awe inspiring upheavals of nature that Galvadon had ever seen. From the East swirled a colossal tornado, its diameter was as wide as the entire city. From the West thundered a wall of water the height of a mountain. From the North a massive volcano erupted spewing a river of lava. From the South, the ground cracked open swallowing everything in its path.

"We cannot fight the Elements but we can fight the men controlling them," Wardek howled calling his pack to him and the wolves charged the Elite.

"Not so fast." The Karakan stood in front of the Elite and raised the Master's Blade protectively. The wolves bounced off an invisible shield the sword had created around the Elite. As long as they were under the protection of the sword, the Elite were untouchable. The Karakan laughed, "When will they ever learn?"

The outer cities were destroyed first and then tornado and lava destroyed the great wall around the city and the tsunami and fissure swallowed up every structure in inside it. Half of Galvadon was wiped out and in moments there would be nothing left. The people began to panic.

"Do not be afraid," shouted Jonuke climbing up to the highest point on the rubble. "He cannot hurt us if we band together. Yes, the Elite are powerful, but there are more of us than they." At Jonuke's command, the Supreme Council shifted their Elements to hold back the destruction, but they were no match for the combined power of four squads of trained Elite and were only able to slightly slow the devastation. The Elementals began to argue with one another about how to proceed.

"Ha!" the Karakan scoffed. "Do you hear yourself, Drek? You'll never get them to work together. They are far more interested in bickering than even saving their own lives."

"The council cannot do this alone," Jonuke shouted to the Elementals. "Galvadon will be destroyed if you cannot let go of your pride and cooperate. Pyrosians, you must redirect the lava into the crevice." Immediately, Falnor followed Jonuke's order and tried to divert the lava. The Pyrosians looked around like they weren't sure what to do. Who was this Vanguard? Why should they listen to him?

Truen climbed up next to Jonuke. "Do as he says!" he shouted and joined Falnor in redirecting the lava which began to slightly shift course. When the Pyrosians saw their success, more joined the fight and were able to completely divert the river of lava into the gap in the earth.

"Good!" shouted Jonuke. "Now Hydrans, direct the flood water into the crevice to cool the lava. Oregg and Yondel immediately followed Jonuke's instruction and the other Hydrans followed.

The Aerisians worked to reverse the flow of the tornado while the Terrans raised a bank of earth to help contain the flood water and lava and divert them away from the city. The Elementals began to see that when they worked together they could accomplish something great.

"It's working!" an Elemental shouted. And murmurs of joy and relief spread through the crowd.

"Stop them, Silvane!" the Karakan bellowed.

Silvane turned his attention on the Elementals and began to shake the earth beneath their feet. The people reeled to and fro and lost their concentration. With no resistance, the destructive Elements turned back toward Galvadon.

Fearing for their own safety and that of their families, the people ran for higher ground. "Now all of Galvadon has witnessed your complete failure, Vanguard," the Karakan mocked.

Just then Granny saw the Freemen signaling her from the woodland just beyond the Citadel's remains. Her eyes glinted with mischief as she turned to the Karakan and yelled, "Don't be so sure, you squd-chewin' gristle smoocher."

"What did you just call me?" the Karakan seethed turning to face Granny. As he did so, he unwittingly lowered the Master's Blade, thereby removing its protection over the Elite. The Freemen used the distraction to reposition themselves and take aim at the Elite with their blow guns.

"A droopy-drawered scum licker," replied Granny.

"That's not what you said the first time," countered the Karakan.

"You're right, the first time I meant to call you a pea-brained skunk sniffer," Granny quipped with delight.

Silvane looked around in confusion as several of his men grabbed their necks and fell to the ground. With the Elite weakened, the tornado began to peter out, the flood started to dwindle, the fracturing earth slowed significantly, and the volcano gradually fizzled.

"What's happening?" the Karakan demanded. "Don't stop now!"

Silvane bent and pulled a dart out of one guard's neck, "They've been sleep darted."

"But how?" the Karakan asked.

"With the help from the brothers of RoR, the Remnant of the Rhonnadon," Londor said leading the Freemen out of the woodland. They were followed by Nya and Scithe's family. A cheer went up among the Elementals at the fortuitous turn of events.

"Now is our chance! Recommence the defensive maneuvers!" Jonuke shouted. "Fight for Galvadon!" Silvane again tried to attack the people but Jonuke shifted a massive shield over the entire population and the Terran's attempts were thwarted. With the power of the Elite lessened, the Elementals renewed their counterattack. In minutes, the catastrophic annihilation of Galvadon had ceased.

"Don't give up, you cowards!" the Karakan bellowed. But the Elite were no longer listening to him. They had seen what Jonuke had done for Galvadon and they wanted to be a part of it.

"This can't be happening!" the Karakan raged. "Silvane, do something."

Even the ever loyal Silvane knew that they had been beaten and refused to fight. "The Vanguard is too powerful. He has done the impossible. He has united Galvadon."

"But I have the Crown of Rulers!" The Karakan turned to the crowd of Elementals and pointed to his crown. "You must all bow to me as your ruler."

"Have you noticed your crown is missing a gem?" asked Truen. "Maybe that's your problem."

"Argh!" The Karakan was furious. "Have you all forgotten that I hold the Master's Blade? No one can stand against its power, my power. Not even the Vanguard with all of his unity."

Taeliah stepped out of the crowd. "The Master's Blade was never meant to be a weapon of destruction but one of defense. If we do not fight back, you have no power over us."

"That can't be true ...." Karakan's face went white. He realized he had always had the muscle of the Elite behind him. With them gone, the Master's Blade was useless.

Jonuke made his way over to the Karakan. "It's over Dendrid. You have no more power here," Jonuke declared. "Leave Galvadon and never return," he finished quietly.

Dendrid turned as if he was going to walk away. *You Jonuke of Londor!* He seethed. *You are responsible for this! If I cannot rule Galvadon, then no one will. If nothing else, this is still a sword.* Suddenly, he whirled around and swung the Master's Blade at Jonuke.

"Jonuke!" Nya screamed, but it was too late. The Karakan's blade slammed against Jonuke's shoulder with deadly force. However, in that instant, the dragon scale's mission was fulfilled as it multiplied into hundreds of scales at the point of impact. The indestructible scales shattered the sword into a thousand pieces. The Karakan looked disbelievingly at the fragments of his all-powerful blade.

"You know what, buddy?" Granny said eyeing the remaining section of the mural. "We've asked you to leave nicely. Now, really, it's time to go." She plucked the crown off the Karakan's head and gave him a big shove. Flailing clumsily, the Karakan fell into the painting and disappeared.

All eyes went to Silvane who looked uneasily at the people of Galvadon, not seeing one friendly face. M'lai walked over to him and said, "You were a cruel husband, Silvane. You separated me from my son. You have made us fugitives in our own land. But it is over now. I have my family and I am happy. I can see that you will never be happy and for that I am sorry for you. I don't believe this will mean anything to you, but it does to me. I forgive you."

Silvane looked at the people he had personally hunted down, the people he had hurt. He looked at his daughter, Iliana. He hadn't known about her, and he thought that had probably been for the best. All the things M'lai had said about him were true, but she was wrong about one thing. Her forgiveness had meant something to him. He turned and jumped into the painting following the Karakan into the Darke Forest. He had followed him for so long, he didn't know how to do anything different.

Nya walked through the crowd to Jonuke. "We found the missing kingdom," she beamed proudly. "It's M'lai and Iliana." She nodded to Iliana who took the star-shaped gem from her necklace and gave it to

Jonuke. Granny handed Jonuke the crown and he put the last gem in place.

As soon as he did, there was a bright flash of light and Mahlneer appeared before the people. A murmur of excitement and awe rippled through the onlookers. *Was that really Mahlneer? The great ruler of Galvadon.* They wondered.

"Jonuke of Londor, you have found all the gems and united the Elementals," declared Mahlneer. "By this you have shown you are ready to lead this people into an era of peace and prosperity. I hereby crown you, Jonuke of Londor, Ruler of Galvadon." He placed the Crown of Rulers on Jonuke's head and Jonuke's appearance transformed before their eyes.

His clothing changed from drab Drek attire to a kingly cream colored suit with gold trim and buttons. His shiny black boots came to his knees. A cream and gold trimmed cloak covered his shoulders and the Crown of Rulers rested on his brow. The shattered Master's Blade pieced itself back together and then sheathed itself in the scabbard at his waist. Jonuke truly looked like a king.

Every knee bent out of respect for and in honor their new ruler. "All hail the Vanguard, the true ruler of Galvadon!" Mahlneer shouted.

Then all rose to their feet and followed suit, chanting. "All hail the Vanguard! All hail the Vanguard! All hail the Vanguard, the true ruler of Galvadon!"

Londor and Linayah's eyes met for the first time since her disappearance. "Linayah?!" Londor shouted pushing his way through the throng. "You're alive?" he said taking her in his arms. "I assumed the worst."

"All is right again, my love. Galvadon is at peace and we are a family once more," she said as he took her in his arms and then kissed her soundly on the lips.

"And it's about time," Fantisma announced. "I'd say it's high time we invited the Rhonnadon back to Galvadon."

"You know of the Rhonnadon?" Jonuke asked.

"Know them? I am one of them. I was sent to keep an eye on Dendrid and Linayah without getting involved. When they snuck away, it was a sign to the Rhonnadon that the time of the Vanguard was near."

"If you are Rhonnadonian, why do I not recognize you?" Linayah asked suspiciously.

"You don't know your Aunt Fanny?" Fantisma asked removing her white frizzy dandelion wig and revealing a head full of red frizzy hair.

"Aunt Fanny!" Linayah chuckled and hugged her aunt.

Jonuke turned to the crowd. "What say you Galvadon? Are you ready to welcome the Rhonnadon home?" A cheer went up through the crowd.

"Just say the words, 'Rhonnadon come home,'" Fanny instructed.

"Rhonnadon," Jonuke said deliberately, "come home." The rubble that was Galvadon transformed as Jonuke had. Where the Citadel had been the lost castle of the Rhonnadon now stood and the ruined city was changed into beautiful homes and buildings much like the ones Jonuke had seen among the Rhonnadon.

The Rhonnadon materialized in front of the castle and immediately began introducing themselves to the people that they had longed to meet.

Gannon hugged Jonuke heartily and said, "Thank you for bringing us home Jonuke. You have fulfilled your destiny. May there always be peace and prosperity in Galvadon."

Epilogue

When the dust settled, there were big changes in Galvadon. The Rhonnadon set about teaching the people of the old ways and Galvadon began to function much like he had seen in the Forgotten Kingdom. The people continued to learn to work together to accomplish great things and learned to develop additional talents.

The seven other kingdoms returned to their homes with a great respect for Galvadon's ruler and an affinity for its people. Highways between the kingdoms were built and trade flourished. Some even came to live in Galvadon and set up places of business like the dwarves' "Towers are Us" that promised the tallest structures in the land and the gnomes' "Gnome-made Clothing Store." To Yondel's delight, the Tornado Tuesday Cleaning Service became available to all Galvadonians.

Mahlneer and his wife Pinay were often seen visiting the castle at Jonuke's request. Jonuke had a lot of questions about ruling Galvadon. Mahlneer made sure Jonuke understood what *not* to do as well as what *to* do. On one of these trips, Mahlneer ran into Phrip who Jonuke had asked to stay on. The tearfully contrite and grateful Phrip happily agreed to his new assignment as Jonuke's personal assistant.

Mahlneer mistook Phrip for his long lost son Phrenon. As it turned out Phrenon was Phrip's great-great- granddaddy. Phrip produced a journal that recounted how much Phrenon had respected and loved his father. Mahlneer was finally able to rest in peace.

Scithe built a beautiful new home for his family where they lived in peace and joy for many years. Scithe proved to be a little overprotective and was often seen morphing into a rock beast and chasing away Iliana's potential suitors.

Renden and Edween (aka Granny) discovered they had quite the affinity for one another. However, when Renden suggested that they court, Granny refused. "I'm not gettin' any younger. Let's get this show on the road." They were married the next day.

Londor, Linayah, and Sheezu moved to the castle to be with Jonuke. Sheezu retired from hunting and lived in the lap of luxury enjoying his platter that never ran out of steak and giving children rides around the city.

From the day they were reunited, Londor and Linayah never left each other's side. They opened a school for the former Drek to educate them about their gifts. Renden was their first student and was delighted to discover he had the rare gift for healing.

Yondel, having overcome her resentment for Scithe, was able to remember everything about her parents with the help of her magical hairbrush. She learned that her father had always wanted her to remember that if she closed her eyes and let her mind travel back to Palean, she would always be able to see him and her mother and feel of their love for her, which she did often. Yondel and Truen continued to flirt for several more years until one day he popped the question. As it turned out, Valent had also proposed to Taeliah and they planned a double wedding.

The Galvadonians learned that when Elementals intermarried, their gifts became even stronger. The contention had ended, but a healthy sense of competition remained which proved quite entertaining at the annual Galvadonian Games that now included all of the nine kingdoms which made for a very interesting show.

As for Jonuke and Nya, they became the best of friends and enjoyed long walks in the forest together. After many years and when both were no longer adverse to the thought of marriage, their friendship matured into love and to Gannon's delight, they were married. He immediately began hounding them about grandchildren.

The piece of mural was kept in the library as a reminder of what Galvadon had been and after all, Dendrid was still a member of the family. From time to time Jonuke would stop by the rock in the library and check on his uncle. Sometimes he would give him updates on how Galvadon was progressing. Other times he would watch as he and Silvane ran from the screechers, hornets, and scorpions that were in there with them and wonder what had led him to this sad existence. But Jonuke would never leave without asking Dendrid if he was ready to come out yet, but the Karakan seemed to prefer his little self-made prison to a life of peace and prosperity.

Jonuke was a wise leader who was well-loved by all who knew him. He made sure to follow Mahlneer's advice and never let greed make his choices and Shayzah's advice to protect the people's agency. Eventually, he even won the fairy queen over.

Jonuke ruled for many years as did his son and his son's son, but most importantly, Galvadon had learned a great lesson about trust, unity, and the Rhonnadonian way.

Own all four books in the Vanguard Series!

About the Author

Julie loves a project. She has dabbled in a variety of ventures from furniture upholstery and triathlon racing to home renovation and "Jerry-rigging" anything that squeaks, cracks, or sags. By far her most challenging undertaking has been the writing the Vanguard Series, where she seeks to transport her readers to thrilling adventures in new worlds. As an elementary teacher, she often rewards her students' good behavior with dramatic re-tellings of her childhood adventures. This was where she first discovered her flare for storytelling. She lives in Mesa, Arizona with her husband, Scott, and their eight children.

Made in the USA
San Bernardino, CA
30 January 2020